LUCKY

SARAH LEAMY

Copyright 2011
All rights reserved — Sarah Leamy

No part of this book may be reproduced or transmitted in any form or by any means, graphic, electronic, or mechanical, including photocopying, recording, taping, or by any information storage retrieval system, without the permission, in writing, from the publisher.

Copyright 2016 (Second Edition) - Sarah Leamy
CreateSpace Publishers

With Thanks

I write for myself, but then when I finish and offer these stories to the world beyond my cabin in the hills, I realize I'm surrounded with such incredible support; even though my brother, his kids, my cousins, aunts and uncles are all still in Britain, I also have another kind of family here in New Mexico. And so my thanks are to you, the crazy making freaks, musicians, writers, homesteaders, kids, fire-fighters, and friends of Madrid, new Mexico.

Much love.

PART ONE

1

I started out with nothing. I still have most of it left.

Dad had met my mom in the sixties in the San Francisco Bay area. He was a 21-year-old army boy, she a street kid, following the hippie myth all the way from Higginsville, Missouri. One night. One kid. A lucky kid. That's what they'd told me.

Dad did the right thing. Mom didn't. She died when I was ten. That wasn't part of the plan. Dad kept me. For a while. And then he couldn't.

They call me Lucky. My parents that is, they called me Lucky when I was a kid. Anyway, there I was, in my late thirties, wondering what the hell to do with myself. My dad, my girlfriend, my dog, my job, and my best friend; all were gone. For one reason or another, I'd lost them all. I stayed in Santa Fe. I tried to work, to keep the homestead fires going, but, well, like I said, it was a rough year. I packed my bags, threw everything into the crew cab of my 1983 Nissan truck, and prayed she would take me further than Eldorado, the one in Santa Fe, that is. With camera in hand, I looked for a new life.

Is this what they call a mid-life crisis?

2

I don't like people. Or rather—I didn't. I had reason enough not to. I liked watching. I liked listening to them. Sometimes I even talked to them, laughed, and enjoyed myself. But, on the whole, I didn't like people. That's not to say I haven't loved. Deeply. I have. I even liked some of my lovers. But usually it was a mix of love and hate. It made it easier to leave that way. I'd always been the first to leave. Until Susan. She left me. Suddenly. Shockingly. So much for that relationship.

I'd woken up one morning, a Sunday morning, and she wasn't there, next to me, asleep. She'd gone. It had been one of those nights that I'd taken a sleeping pill mixed with four pints of ale. I'd slept deeply for once.

Susan apparently made the most of it.

I was impressed, in a way, by her quiet, cold thoroughness. She took the photos off the walls, ones of us five years earlier in Ireland on the coast, laughing and hugging. She took the water color landscape, a painting I'd given her, one my dad had painted when a teenager in Michigan. Did she know even then that he wasn't coming home from the hospital? She took her favorite coffee mug. All gone. She left me her dirty laundry. Thanks. I loved your dirty socks, Susan. Most definitely how I would choose to remember you.

Like I said, it was a Sunday morning, around ten o'clock, when I finally pulled myself out of the deep depressive fog of a fake night's sleep. The curtains were drawn. Did I do that? Blue, my dog, sat up and yawned. Groggily, I sat up and reached for a t-shirt and shorts, pulled them on, then walked out the hall to the bathroom. I hung my head over the sink. Cold water was what I craved. I drank. I soaked. I shook my hair out. And then I looked around.

Gone. Far Gone.

Written on the mirror in maroon lipstick were the words she left for me. Scrawled really, it was barely legible. I opened the medicine cabinet to find the shelves empty. No more make-up, toothbrushes or moisturizer, nothing left. Not even my shampoo, Head and Shoulders Original. I closed the door and reread Susan's message.

Gone. Far Gone.

I crossed my arms. I almost screamed. Instead I banged my head against the mirror. My eyes watered. I lay on the floor of the bathroom and stared, empty at last. I heard a knock at the front door. Blue barked. I heard the slap of the doggy door as she let herself out back. I stared. Nothing. I heard nothing. I felt nothing. Better that way.

When I finally came downstairs, a note lay next to the front door, slipped through the crack, my own form of air conditioning, those cracks and leaks around the doors and windows were. I opened the envelope.

Hey Lucky. Not such a good day for you, eh? I got a text from Susan saying she'd left you again. For good this time. Has she? Give me a call. Thought I'd buy you a beer or three at the Cowgirl. Mike.

I rested the note on the kitchen table and put on the kettle for coffee. Normalcy through these simple actions, right? Wake up. Drink coffee. Smoke. Wash. Get dressed. Walk the dog. Pretend life is the same as yesterday. Yeah right, I watched the coffee drip through the filter. I added cream and one sugar. I stared at the note and looked around the kitchen. Subtle changes. I looked back at the mug in front of me. Mine. My favorite striped mug. Blue sat at my feet, waiting for a walk, waiting for me to notice her. I hardly did. Should I go for a beer with Mike? Or go back to bed and hope to wake up only to find Susan in bed curled up next to me? Or maybe I'd hear her in the kitchen, making herself a cup of tea?

When I woke back up, the message still greeted me in the bathroom. Mike's note still sat on the table. And Susan was still gone, far gone. I pulled out the camera. *Click.* Nothing had changed. Well, I had. I felt cold. Deeply and darkly angry. A beer wouldn't be a good idea. Not right now. I found the long green leash and talked to Blue as we walked up the road, she stopping to sniff and pee, then coming with me, finally. When I took her back home, I fed her wet food, a bribe for ignoring her all day. I put the bowl down in the kitchen by the hot water heater and she looked at me suspiciously. A smart dog, but then again, what did I expect from a Border Collie? I petted her and closed the door behind me, zipping up the leather once again. I went to find Mike. It was Sunday after all. That was what we did on Sundays; we'd meet for a beer and a laugh with the boys at the bar.

3

Mike is tough, fearless and short. About five foot five. We all thought he'd have a late growth spurt, but no, he didn't. Being tough became his defense. A fighter, that's Mike. And a lover, always in with the girls. I don't know how he does it, but he does. He's not pretty or handsome by any standards. And when we were teens living on the army base near Oxford in England, we'd had a few fights. He won. And then he'd buy me a pint. Two years older than me, he got the beers and the girls. Lucky bugger. But it changed. He'd been on his own since that divorce a few years ago. Wife took the kids back to Europe. He chose to stay here in New Mexico.

A regular Sunday at the bar, that's what I'd wanted. I walked up Manhattan Street, across the railroad tracks, past Second Street's new downtown place (too much like waiting at a train station for my liking) and up Guadalupe to the Cowgirl. More my style. Four small dark rooms with wood floors, random tables, and cowboys both real dusty and touristy clean, yep; a mix of locals and tourists makes for a good variety of entertainment. Distraction. Oh, and the best margaritas in town. I put out the smoke, and stepped into the dark bar, camera in hand. *Click.* Mike sat at the far end, chatting to Laura, the newest bartender to join the scene. She laughed out loud as she looked over to me. I came up to Mike, taking off my leather.

"Pale Ale, Lucky?" and she held up a pint glass, ready to pour me one. I nodded and sat at the stool to Mike's left.

"Hey, buddy." He tipped his pint toward me and grinned. "So you finally emerged then?"

I nodded and drank down the first pint. Laura quickly refilled for me without a word.

"First things first, how's your dad?"

"The same."

We sipped our drinks quietly for a moment. But then he couldn't resist asking. "So she's gone, eh? What did you do this time?"

"Me? Nothing." I shook my head.

"I know you better than that, Lucky, and you know it. Let me ask you again. What did you do this time?" Mike took a gulp from his Guinness.

I took a taste of pint number two. It did wonders for my mood. Although Mike wouldn't let up with his questions.

"Where is she? What happened to Susan?" He grinned widely, teeth crooked and an odd shade of nicotine and stout. You can see why I never understood his success with the girls.

"All I know is that she left me a note on the mirror, saying 'Gone, all gone.' Not sure why. She's taken all her stuff. Photos, clothes, books, boots, but not her dirty laundry. I have her socks on the bedroom floor. Thoughtful of her, eh?"

"Oh, I'm sorry, Lucky. Do you know where she's gone this time? Is it someone else?"

"It's Abra."

Mike looked stunned. "She never told me about Abra. Who's that? I've never heard the name. Are you sure? Who is she?" He acted as jealous as I felt.

"Abra is an Alpaca in Spain."

Mike's look of relief turned into laughter. "You're joking, right?" He looked at me and then around the bar. It was filling up with the brunch crowd, here to see the Gospel Americana music on the weekends. I stared over the counter and took in the game on the television. Just starting up for another college game. Not my thing, to be honest. But distractions can be great. At the bar to my side, I noticed five locals, chatting away, taking bets on who'll win, and ordering more beers. Yep, nothing had changed.

I drank my pint and stood up to go smoke on the patio. Cold outside, definitely warm-jacket weather, but could be much worse considering it was almost Halloween. At the table under the propane heater sat an older couple, in their fifties perhaps; he read the New York Times, she had a book in hand. No words spoken between them as I smoked. Had they been together that long they didn't need to speak any more? Or was it boredom? I couldn't decide if I was jealous of them or relieved to be single again.

I turned back inside and sat with Mike. He looked over at me but said nothing. Have we known each other that long? No words needed? Like the old married couple?

I offered what I had to tell. "Abra is an Alpaca in Seville. I guess she's gone there. Remember we went there last spring? Susan loved it, the heat, and the smells of the pine trees baking in the midday sunshine, the animals on the farm, the kids chasing each other across the beaches, the campfires at night under the clear skies. Yeah, I hadn't seen Susan that relaxed for ages. Abra was born when we were staying at this one farm out in the hills near Seville. The second morning we woke up to hear excited chattering and footsteps hurrying back and forth across the cobblestone yard. Susan pulled on shirt, shorts and boots and headed out to find out what was going on. She ran back in an hour later, breathless and shining, full of life and energy and she practically dragged me out to this pen beyond the barn. She said, 'isn't she beautiful? I watched her being born, I helped the mama and now look, she's on her feet already. It's amazing. Have you ever seen anything born, Lucky?' I shook my head. Susan's white t-shirt and blue jeans were splattered with blood and dirt. I could hardly look at her. She babbled on and on about the magic of it all, the slime and blood and hoofs and head and afterbirth and I cringed. I don't like blood. Glad I'd stayed in the cottage and had my coffee. 'We're calling her Abra, it means magical.' Susan had hugged me and kissed me deeply. 'Lets go home, Lucky,' she'd said. 'Let's celebrate!' And we'd spent the rest of the day in the cottage until the baby alpaca took her away from me later that afternoon."

I laughed bitterly and thought of all the great sex with her, oh, and the constant fights we had about sex. Never satisfied, was she? It always boils down to sex in some way or another, I told Mike.

He ordered a huge plate of nachos for us both, toasted me and then made me eat. "I agree, sex is the killer. But an alpaca, my friend, is not the problem. You need protein. I know you won't eat anything at home. Anyway, tell me the rest."

I sat back. I didn't have much else to add. "Susan left me for that bloody baby alpaca."

"Don't you call them kids?"

"What?"

"Kids. Baby alpacas are called kids," said Mike in all earnestness.

4

We sat at the bar, a long copper counter top over the wooden frame, our jackets hung underneath from the hooks provided. My boots rested on the ledge. The lights were dim and I looked out past the rows of tequila bottles in the window. Literally five rows crammed full of different kinds of tequila. From four dollars to twenty a shot. Incredible.

"Are you sure she left you for the Alpacas? She never said anything to me about that."

Another round or two later, Mike and I still trying to make sense of Susan's disappearance. He was surprised in many ways, knew we'd been struggling, but said he was still surprised.

"Are you sure there isn't someone else?"

I shook my head. "Nah, I would've known, seen her flirting with someone. It's a small town here, isn't it? Can't hide much."

Mike looked relieved. "Glad you know better then. Most people are going to spread rumors, you know? Say she met someone behind your back, was having an affair, that kind of thing."

"You reckon?"

He shrugged. "Just don't believe everything you're told." He caught Laura's attention and asked for the tab.

'Lets go back to my place. You up for it?"

"Yeah, why not?"

We stood up, a little wobbly after the last four hours inside, but okay for a walk to Galisteo Road, not far by any standards. It felt good to be out and about.

The sun was creeping down. The clocks had to change soon, next week maybe? I couldn't remember. I started to light another smoke, but changed my mind and pocketed them, wanting to breathe the winter crisp air for once. Time to stop? Who knew?

We walked down Aztec Street, past the brightly painted funky café, now closed, and up onto Cerrillos. Both of us were silent. I remember wondering what Mike was thinking about, but I never did ask him much. I figured he'd tell me if he wanted to. I looked around the quiet streets of Santa Fe and thought about leaving, taking my dog and my stuff and just leaving. I smiled to myself at the thought. I knew how to leave. It's all Dad taught me. He wouldn't mind if he knew. As an army brat, that was what I knew best, how to pack up the basics and start again somewhere new. A new story to be told. A new self to show. Simple: Drive and start again.

Mike opened the front door and walked into his kitchen. The white walls turned harsh under the lights. He pulled out some cold pepperoni pizza from the fridge and offered me a slice. We stood there and ate in silence.

"Want to talk about your dad? Or Susan?" he asked.

I shook my head. I walked into the living room and crouched down to make a fire. I tore up the Reporter into strips, covered them with kindling from the lumberyard, and built us a fire. Mike turned on a lamp or two in the corners by the windows. I sat back on my haunches. My knees ached but it felt good to stare at the flames. I had no more words. Mike passed me a bottle of Pale Ale, and he sat behind me on the green sofa. He flicked on the television, found the game, and settled in for the night. Good friends, we don't need to say much. He knew me. He knew how much I'd liked Susan. How crappy life had been for the last few weeks. I relaxed and sat back.

"Thanks, Mike."

"For what?" He sounded surprised and I felt him move around behind me.

"Well, for not making a big deal about this. Just some beers, knowing what to say, well, you know me, Mike. Susan. I liked her more than most. I didn't see this coming. But, here I am. Single again. Like you, right?"

"Right."

We drank quietly. The game took our attention for the next three or four hours. Tight at the end, with points up for grabs and into overtime, that final play was what I needed. Distraction. Perfect.

5

I shook out my scruffy brown hair, scratching it as I do. It felt good to be inside. I took off the leather jacket and sat down just as a short mousy blond girl came up with a pad in hand. She wore a pale green uniform with an old black apron full of notepads and pens.

"Aren't you freezing?" She looked out at my truck with its window wide open (or is it missing?), the broken windshield, and the front dashboard covered with a fine layer of snow. She shivered. "Coffee to start?"

I grinned widely. "Is it always this cold in November?"

"Oh, yeah. We usually get the first snow around Halloween. Wisconsin's pretty cold from here on out. Where you from?"

New Mexico, I told her, looking for work, or at least something new to do for the winter. She poured me a deep mug of black coffee and told me she'd ask around of the locals, see who was hiring in town. A late breakfast sounded perfect to me, so I made my order and off she went. I watched as she chatted to the old geezers at the counter, and one by one they turned to check me out. I nodded and drank and picked up the paper. I pulled out the camera without thinking, just habit. *Click.*

The Isthmus gave me a ton of local and national stories. I was impressed by the amount of, well, progressive ideas they had. I'd sort of thought it'd be more of a conservative stronghold, being the Midwest and all, and especially after that little encounter I'd just had in Iowa. I guess the student population defined so much of what went on in Madison that the tea-party freaks were outnumbered here. This was a progressive city beyond all I'd hoped for. I was glad. I don't do well with the right wing folks in the Midwest. They tend to end up screaming at me. I usually walked away when possible, but I have been known to throw a beer mug or two. And even crash a truck on the way out of town.

I read about a recent spate of suicides by young queer kids and I felt for them. I knew all about it, not fitting in. The bullies. The taunts. And the hopelessness. Anyway, the paper talked of how some places like East Lansing, or rather Michigan, was pretty behind the times as far as hate crimes go. In Madison, the overall culture was incredibly liberal; it was almost a sin to be straight. Hate crimes were not to be dismissed here, a zero tolerance policy. But then again, I reckon all crimes are hateful. Not exactly a sign of affection, are they? I mused.

I put the paper down, half into the Culture section when my two eggs, bacon and hash browns showed up. The waitress refilled my coffee mug and sat down. I was surprised. I mean, I'd heard that folks could be friendly, but this? I held my fork and waited. She smiled nervously, put the hair behind her ears, and passed me the salt and pepper before speaking.

"My friend over there," she nodded over to a table near the door that had a single woman in her twenties sitting with a pile of books in front of her, "Chris, she asked me to tell you…oh, this is embarrassing, she asked if you had somewhere to stay." And the waitress blushed deep burgundy, anxiously plucking and tucking her hair, while looking up at me and over to her 'friend.'

"I just got into town a few moments ago. Not sure what I'm doing to be honest. Why?"

She told me that they were roommates, students together at the school, political science and teaching majors between them, and well, they had space if I needed something.

"Oh, well. I don't know." I grabbed my mug and drank it down. I didn't like attention of this kind. Not sure how to respond, so I didn't.

She stood up fast, almost knocking the table and the coffee pot, but she recovered quickly. "Well, we thought we'd offer. Er, here's our number. We're just east of here, up in the Willy Street area. It's kind of fun up there. I like it." And she blushed again as she half- ran to the kitchen.

I looked over quickly to the friend, who raised her mug as a toast to me, one eyebrow lifted and a smile loitering behind a cautious wave. I smiled. I couldn't help it. I smiled and toasted her back. But then I focused on the meal in front of me. I ate it all down fast. Warming myself with good home-cooked potatoes and some good eggs. I loved it.

    I sat back in the booth, finally satiated and relaxed. It had been a long drive, stopping only three nights on the way, once in Hooker, Oklahoma, and once in some small back road town in Kansas. The night before, I'd spent in Iowa—well, kind of. Not so much fun. Anyway, I was deeply tired. By everything that had happened. And my neck was stiff, too. Whiplash?

6

"Excuse me."

I looked up to see the roommate holding her pile of books, gesturing to the seat opposite me. She wore baggy clothes, jeans and a thick padded coat, and was five feet five by my guess, with pale skin and soft smiling eyes, half hidden by the woolen hat and scarf. She pulled them off self-consciously. "Can I sit down a minute? Before you go?"

"Sure. Why not?" I was done eating and curious as to why she'd sent her roommate to talk to me. "How can I help?"

"Christine." And she reached across the table to shake my hand. Oh, polite here. We don't usually do that in Santa Fe, more of a subtle head nod in the right direction.

"Lucky."

We shook. I looked again. She had deep blue eyes, almost the color of a New Mexican sky, but not quite. Straw colored hair, short and rough around the edges. Home. She reminded me of home. She held my hand a moment too long and I sat back quickly.

"Oh, right." Flustered by my sudden move, she reached for my coffee and finished it, and then realized what she'd done. More embarrassment, which made me laugh out loud. Both of us awkward beyond normal dictates.

"Let's start again, shall we? My name's Lucky. Seriously. It's on my driver's license. Want to see?" I started to delve into the leather's inside pocket but Christine said she'd trust me.

"Christine Rose."

"First name and middle name? Last name?"

"Middle name of Rose. My mom's a true romantic. She thought it would get me married by the time I was twenty-one."

"And did it?"

Christine laughed, brushed a hand across her hair and shook her head. "Thankfully, no! I wouldn't be here if it had."

I pulled out my tobacco and started to roll myself one. Her eyes widened in surprise. "I didn't know people still smoked those!"

"Really? What do they smoke, then?"

"Well, to be honest, most of my friends just don't. Never have. Don't you read the newspapers?" She caught herself before she said more. I grinned and put it away. I'd been thinking of cutting back, maybe now was the right time? Christine settled into the booth more comfortably while glancing at her cell phone. She put the five or six books on the bench beside her.

"What have you got there?"

She looked down at them, and then back to me. "Mostly population demographics. There's a lot in the news these days about being Green, right? Well, no one talks about the over-population of the whole world, how it's seriously messing things up and there's not much point wearing used clothes or recycling bottles if we're all killing the planet by having babies just to feed our egos." She paused and sat back.

"Well, now I see why you didn't want to get married and have kids!" I smiled, unable to help myself from teasing this odd woman in front of me. "When I arrived in Madison, I hadn't thought about the pressures of over-population. Just where to warm up. Very selfish of me, I know. What makes it that important to you?"

She reached up to her hair again. "I just cut it," she explained, "it feels weird, to say the least! Still getting used to it, I guess. Anyway, it makes me crazy to see people being all righteous about collecting water in a fifty gallon bucket, recycling their wine bottles, sending ten dollars to Honduras, and then having four or five kids only to send them to expensive private schools, and then each kid gets married and has another four or five kids. It's all mixed up." She waved to the waitress with my empty cup. "I get angry because all this information has been out there for decades. I came across these books by Professor David Smith, from here in Madison. Do you know him? Well, he wrote about the migration, population geography, and how we're depleting the world's resources at ridiculous rates. He wrote all of that back in the '80s! And still, no one's talking about it!" She sat back again as the coffee pot appeared. I took a photo. Unthinkingly. She didn't notice.

"Is she preaching about the evils of having too many children?" The waitress nudged her friend and handed her another mug. "Here you are, Chris. More coffee before the big test. Are you ready?"

Christine laughed at herself. "Yeah, I think I covered the basics, right, Lucky? Oh, this is Joanna; she's all about early childhood development. Part-time reluctant waitress."

"Interesting choice of roommates." They shrugged, and then each reached to tidy up stray hairs, and glance around the room. Christine broke the silence.

"So, how was the trip out here? Did you caught in that storm in Iowa? I'd heard it was a white-out blizzard. The news said there were quite a few crashes on the Interstate."

We all glanced over at the wreck of a truck out the window.

"I pulled into Iowa City last night, that's true. I even found a bar or club or something in the warehouse district by chance. I'd just stopped so I could fall asleep in the truck for a while, catch up, you know?" I sipped the coffee and Joanna poured more out of habit. I added cream but no sugar. "It had just started to come down. I sat in the front of the truck and had a smoke before settling in for a nap. Dark, wintry, empty roads, no people around and then I noticed a light on above a doorway, a sign lit up that I couldn't read from where I was so I thought I'd go explore."

Christine sat back and Joanna leaned against the bench with her hip, putting the coffee pot down on the table.

"I walked across the parking lot and saw it was a bar, and so, feeling like a beer, I went inside. Pretty dark, a long bar, a few folks inside but mostly empty. I sat at the bar and ended up chatting to this woman, Ellen—I think that was her name, anyway—we chatted and laughed and told each other wild stories of snowstorms and floods and tornadoes. Fun, you know?" Christine and Joanna nodded for me to continue. " After a while, well, she invited me back to her place for the night. I was supposed to follow her Honda Accord a few miles up the road. I got into my truck and started it up, as she got ready to drive off. I was about to follow her when this big black Ford F250 pulled out and blocked me. Two men got out, mean fuckers, you could see it in how they walked over, a swagger as if they had nothing to fear. They didn't, really. My engine was still running, lights on them, and I put out the smoke, threw it out. They came up and started threatening me, calling me a dirty hippy, fucking girly-boy, and all of that kind of stuff. One of them, the one doing the talking, got closer and told me to get out of town, not to follow that car home, or his friend would beat the shit out of me and he'd watch. *Understood?* No. Not really. And then I slammed the truck into reverse, almost running over his foot, and threw my cold coffee in his face." I looked up and saw the girls both watching me with half smiles and half fear written across their faces. "I sped out of there and took the highway out of town, through the suburbs and onto the country road. Lights came up behind me so I pulled off at the first dirt road I could find and turned off my own lights as I drove full speed down this gravel road. I lost them. But I also lost grip and I slid off the road at a sharp right bend, and rolled the truck." I looked out at the Nissan. "It looks worse than it is. But, hell of a truck, eh? It landed on its wheels and here I am. Broken windows and all. I'm a bit bruised but okay."

Silence. They stared at the truck's bashed in front end and snow covered dented roof.

"Last night?" Christine asked.

"Yeah." I shrugged. "So, you see, your offer of a place to stay is quite the contrast to the last day or so."

"Was it *all* that bad?" said Joanna, eyes wide.

"No," I laughed, "I actually had fun in Oklahoma, staying in a town called Hooker and hanging out with the truckers at this bar next to a Motel 6, hardcore dudes that took me in and fed me and gave me free beers all night long. I got some great photos of them! And the stories they told. I'm amazed they even spoke to me, to be honest—not exactly their style, am I?"

Joanna drifted off to take care of the last two tables and Christine picked up her books, looking at her cell phone again. "Well, I think you're our style! Anyway, I've got to get to class, but after that introduction of yours, you're still welcome to come stay at the madhouse with us."

"Madhouse?"

"Well," added Joanna, on her way past with a jug of water, "it used to be a halfway home for wayward women—it lasted for ages but then the funding fell through and now it's ours. Still a little crazy making. You'll fit in fine."

I looked up sharply, uncertain as to what she meant by that. She carried on.

"We get a lot of people passing through for weeks at a time. It seems we like to pick up strangers at diners and bring them home to meet the family. Well, anyway, we get some pretty interesting stories around the kitchen table. Usually it's just the two of us, since John and Kevin upstairs have their own kitchen, but we see them every so often. Science majors! Not much in common with us. Anyway, want to stay? I can take you over there if we go right now. We have the sofa you can use and a garage for your stuff. The snow's expected to get worse for the next week but then give us a few weeks before the next storm hits for Thanksgiving."

We all turned to look out the window. My poor truck was already covered in an inch of snow by now, including the front seat. The roads were plowed, though, and it was time to move on.

7

I pulled out the black duffel bag from the back seats, and threw it onto the concrete floor near the back door. The garage was a mess, full of bikes, canoes, tennis rackets and bags, tied up and thrown haphazardly. The shelves contained paint cans, tools, bottles and books. I looked around as I claimed a space for myself. A puddle of snow swam slowly toward the driveway. I shook off the leather jacket, swearing to myself about the dirt roads in Iowa and the idiot bigots that fucked up my truck. I sighed and then I pulled out more stuff, the bedding mostly and then the computer bag from under the front seat. My pile of wet belongings grew. I wiped the seats down, dried off the dash and the radio, and promised to give her a good clean later on.

The door opened and Christine leaned out. "I'm off to school for that test! Back around four. Make yourself at home. There's hot water if you want a shower. See you later, Lucky." The door closed behind her.

I picked up my stuff and shook out the last of the rain and snow before hanging up the coat and closing the garage doors. I looked back briefly, to check on my truck parked in the driveway. She looked safe enough, and anyway, who'd want to steal such a wreck?

Inside, the heat sprang to life, humming in the background. I heard footsteps above me on the wooden floors, someone ran down the stairs and out the front door before I had time to call out. The house was now mine. Silent. Warm. Welcoming. It felt like a family home. That made me sad.

I missed my dad. My dog. I even missed Susan for a moment. A very brief moment.

I took my time wandering from room to room, looking at the bookshelves, the photos and the sorry pile of firewood by the open fireplace in the living room. Four logs at the most. My new bed, the sofa, beckoned to me.

"Not yet, my friend, not yet." I patted the cushions and headed for the bathroom. "Good, a plug means a bath. My bath," I muttered out loud to myself as I opened the faucets and checked the temperature. I didn't like bathrooms these days, scared to look in the mirrors. I didn't look. I kept my eyes on the porcelain bathtub, the maroon rug, and shelves of girly lotions. I took out my travel-sized shampoo bottle, the new crisp washcloth and a fresh bar of soap, all straight from the motel in Okie. I stripped out of the worn black jeans and gray shirt, down to the basics I was born with and sat myself with feet in the tub and body stretched out above.

I heard nothing but the taps flowing. It was a beautiful sound. The walls were painted a deep forest green, and the windows were red but with yellow curtains across them, making the room strangely dark. I pulled them open and I glanced out only to see the blue wooden house next door. A tall dark-haired woman stood out on her porch, smoking and watching me. I nodded. She smiled. And then walked inside.

The snow kept falling. I was here to stay.

I unpacked the clean jeans, a book (*Blue Highways*—it seemed appropriate) and sat down in front of the fire I'd just made. A time to breathe for myself and not be running on adrenalin or rage. I sat back and let my eyes close. No bad dreams yet. I drifted off.

8

I'd come home from work to find Mike at my place, inside and alone. Unusual, to say the least. He had a key, but still. Anyway, I let myself in and threw off the denim onto the kitchen chair. I called out to Blue out of habit and then remembered. She'd gone. Lost in the woods. I stopped, floored for a second by the memory of her running in the trees.

Mike stood in the bedroom door, disheveled, and shocked to see me. Two weeks ago he'd taken me in for a few days after Susan left. He'd listened to me venting for a few days but then he sent me home, telling me it's the best way to get myself together. To be in my own home. To reclaim the space for myself.

And then, there he was, looking like shit, in my house with the doors open, drawers pulled out and laptop on the kitchen table.

"What's wrong, Mike? You okay?" I walked up to him but he pushed past me as if to leave. Without saying anything. I held him, grabbed his shoulder. "What you doing here, Mike? In my bedroom? What's going on? Why's my stuff scattered around?"

He shook me off, and then he turned back to me. Stared at me before speaking words I'd not expected.

"Susan told me to get the photos you took."

"What photos? Why?" I didn't get it. I stood close. Too close even for my liking. "Mike?"

"The ones you took of her sleeping. Her naked. In the bath with you. All of them. She doesn't want you to have them. Where's your camera?"

I didn't touch the pocket. He should know by now where I keep it. On me. At all times. "But they're my photos. Not hers. And definitely not yours. What's going on, Mike?"

"She doesn't want you to look at them."

"But she'll let you? What the hell, Mike?" I turned away from him and walked to the fridge, grabbed two pale ales, opened them both and offered him one. That's what you do with friends, right? Share? But not that. Not my girlfriend. I don't share. Never have. Never will. "She knew I had them, knew I kept them," I went on. "It wasn't a big deal."

"Well, it is now, Lucky. I have to delete them for her. Or take the memory stick." He stared me down. "Which will it be?"

Mike drank deeply of his beer, and put the bottle on the wooden table between us. He said nothing more. Waiting for me to reach the obvious conclusion? No. Not me. Not my closest friend.

I walked outside, back onto Manhattan Street and up to the railyard for a beer at Second Street Brewery. He'd never look for me there. He wouldn't come after me. I didn't care what he said to Susan about the photos. I'd keep them. She'd let me take them. I'd do whatever I wanted with them. Anyway, I didn't want to talk to him, to anyone I knew. The winter chill had set in, and the streets were empty. Had he gone onto my computer? It didn't sound like it. And what was he doing with Susan? I sat at the bar, in the corner near the waitresses' staging area. I could see the main doorway, and if pushed, I'd leave through the kitchen. I drank one, then two more beers. I stood out front under a porch at the warehouse next door to smoke. I spoke to no one. I didn't want to go home. I didn't. I pulled out the camera. *Click.*

"Lucky?"

A gentle voice woke me up and I heard her add a log to the fire. I'd slept hard all afternoon. I struggled to untangle myself from the blanket someone had thrown over me, and sat up. Christine squatted on her knees and stared at the flames now sparking and sputtering. She looked up at me and looked away quickly. Too quickly, as if nervous to be around me.

"What?"

She stayed still for a moment and then took off her black knee length coat, telling me I'd cried out in my dreams. And how she'd tried to wake me from the nightmares but I'd pushed her off me, raging and crying until I suddenly lay still. Half an hour she'd watched me sleeping. Unmoving as if deadened. Lost.

I stood up and walked out to the bathroom. I looked at the mirror. No messages for me. I sat on the edge of the bathtub and stared out the window. That woman was over there smoking again, huddled in a coat and scarf, watching the snow swirling around the streetlights. She didn't look my way.

Christine had spread her books on the table.

"What you doing?" I sat down opposite her and pulled a book toward me, glancing at the title, *The Secret Resources*. I put it back. When I looked up finally, she was leaning forward in the chair, holding onto the table between us. She took a deep breath.

"We need to talk."

Ah, not a good phrase in my experience, I told her, trying to make light of the tension. She didn't laugh, only offered me a glimmer of a smile. "Okay, how's this then? Is there something we need to know? Why are you out on the road, Lucky? What happened the other night? It got me worried, is that the kind of thing that happens to you a lot?"

"Mind if I have a cup of coffee? Do you want one?"

"Sure, but I have to study. I'm not planning on sitting here talking with you all night long."

I sat back down, and tried to work out what to say. "I'm just unlucky, I guess." Trying to make light of it. One look at Christine's face told me to stick to the basics, no joking around right now. "Well, it's been a rough year for me. A few weeks ago, I broke up with my girlfriend in Santa Fe. Then I lost my best friend last week, and—I thought I'd travel and go somewhere new for a while. Take photos. Relax, that kind of thing. I didn't kill anyone. Like I said, just not living up to me name." I didn't mention the fight with Mike. I'd hurt him, but she didn't need to know that, did she? Physically, I hurt him. That's all. Last I heard, Mike was out of the hospital, going to the physical therapist, but had some problem with his one knee. Found it difficult to move around freely. "Well, it was time to move on." I finished with that.

"That's it? Honestly? A bad break up?" She stared at me, not blinking, just reading me.

I nodded and looked into my mug. It was empty already. I didn't tell her about Dad. Or Blue. Christine stood and got me another, plus she grabbed the bag of Lays potato chips and poured them into a green bowl. She picked at them as I drank the black coffee down rapidly, hoping to stave off more sleep. Too many nightmares running through my brain. I couldn't let myself dream anymore. I planned to stay up and take photographs. Of anything. Go explore the city, the neighbors, and the bars. Travel and snap away at a new life, a new world around me. Better than staying in Santa Fe amid the rumors and fights, right?

That talk about my crappy relationship softened Christine and she told me how she'd been single for years now, not interested in anyone, too much trouble for her, not easy. She was cynical. And anyway, she preferred her own company, and the books. So many books. I poked the fire and made it flare up brightly before I admitted, "I've always been with someone. I think about it. Being single. But I don't know, I start out thinking I'm just dating, not a big deal. And then years later, like with Susan, I realize I did it again, got involved, moved in, and did everything with her, cooking, working, paying bils, going on vacations. Still thinking I'm single, but not really. This is the first time I'm on my own." I couldn't tell her the rest of the story.

She grinned and grabbed my hand before I could move it. "And how is it? Lonely? Freeing? Which is it? Are you having fun yet?" She let go of me and watched.

I shook my head. "Not so much fun, no, not recently," I told her.

She laughed at my stupidly pitiful expression. "Well, me and Joanna, we know how to play and laugh and eat good food, talk up a storm, and then go to bed alone. Every night we do that. It's amazing, Lucky. I love it. You might even learn to love it."

I doubted it.

"Do you play music?" Christine looked up from her notes, and pushed aside the laptop. She stretched out wide and yawned loudly, finishing with a yelp and a sigh. She sat back, patting the little tummy, her Buddha belly she'd called it earlier, laughing at her self. Her arms hung loosely from her sides, hidden in the Green Bay Packers sweatshirt, as she watched me cutting up the onions. "Are you sure you don't want any help?"

My eyes were dropping water onto the plate of red onions in front of me but I grinned, happy to be cooking in a kitchen again. Quite domestic. "Nah, thanks though. Do you like garlic? Does Joanna?"

"You didn't answer my question, about the music. Do you? I have a guitar but I never play it, not a priority for me right now. Anyway, it's in my bedroom if you want to borrow it."

I shrugged and turned back to the job at hand. "Not a big drive of mine, either."

"What do you to relax, then? Cook?"

"Yep!" I opened the fridge and pulled out the organic ground beef. I grabbed the corncobs while there. I scraped off the kernels and sautéed them with the onions and garlic, adding a touch of ginger and chile peppers. "I hope you like it spicy. I come from New Mexico, after all; I don't know how to cook without peppers." I stirred the skillet once more before adding the meat. It sizzled perfectly and filled the room with a smell that set my stomach grumbling impatiently. I answered her question as I stirred.

"I take photos. When I can't sleep at night, I wander the streets and take photos. Of whatever I see through the lens. Shoot from the hip. Low to the ground, I'll squat and wait at street corners, watch the bars empty out at last call, or I'll hang out near the gas stations and railyards, see who is up and capture them on the Sony." I added the tomatoes and turned down the gas range to simmer.

We were waiting for Joanna to get back from her last class of the night. Dark outside. Cozy inside. Chris and I'd spent the rest of the afternoon walking through the snow to the co-op. We'd picked up supplies since the weather had turned against me, and the likelihood of my leaving in the morning was lessening by the hour. She and I had walked and chatted. She told me of growing up in Cleveland, and how her parents just wanted her happily married and working a nice nine-to-five job in the mall. Not enough for her, she'd left home, worked and then traveled to Europe for a few years before coming back. With the Midwest having some of the worst hit states of the depression—sorry, recession—she realized it was time to go back to school. Either that or be unemployed like all the others. Now she had just turned twenty-eight and was focused on studying. Single, too. Determined to remain single.

Once home, we carried on chatting over a cup of tea as I cooked. She was easy company for me, with no pressure to say that much. Like Mike had been for me. Mike. Yeah. I needed to—what? I didn't know. I didn't know what had happened, not really.

What had I done this time?

The front door opened and Joanna came flying in, her scarf half off, a hat thrown to the floor on her way through. "Gotta pee!" she yelled and off she ran.

Chris rolled her eyes and cleaned the books off the table. I boiled the water for the pasta. I pulled out three bowls.

9

I woke to six inches of snow on the roads and more on the sidewalks. The city had done its job of plowing the roads and now it was up to the residents to clean the rest. I had nothing better to do.

So I bundled up in all my clothes, found a pair of work gloves, and went looking for a snow shovel in the garage. It took a while to uncover it. Where did all that stuff come from? I had to tidy up first. It took a while, like I said.

On the fifth driveway, my energy started to lag. I sat on the curb and looked around. The neighborhood was made up of old wooden houses with wrap-around porches. Sofas and armchairs of all colors and ages were scattered on the decks and even in the yards, with basketballs, bikes and broken down cars lining the driveways. A student enclave if ever I saw one. I relaxed into the sunshine on my face, briefly missing the ever-present New Mexico heat.

"Do you have a light?"

Above me on the front steps stood the tall woman from yesterday, the one who saw me naked in the bathroom. I turned bright red and got up, slipping into the drift I'd just made, landing face forward. A hand reached down and pulled me up by the scruff of the neck, hoisting me upright.

"There you go, Sailor. Steady on your feet."

I'm five nine, not exactly short myself, but she still towered over me. I didn't want to ask or say something stupid, but apparently I couldn't help it. "Fuck me, you're tall!"

She laughed and shrugged. I stumbled backwards. I slipped on the ice. Again. She picked me up again. "Was that a yes?"

"A yes—what?"

"A light," and she held out her slightly crumpled cigarette.

I reached into my jeans and pulled out the tobacco packet and the lighter fell out into the snow. I found it though, pretty fast, and dried it on the scarf and handed it to her.

"Is it always going to be this hard to have a cigarette with you?" She took a deep breath in and looked me up and down. "You look a bit damp there. Want to come in for a cup of tea?"

I looked up at the gray wooden porch with the rocking chair and plant pots lying empty. Christmas lights had been strung across the bay windows. I looked back at Christine's place and I followed her inside, quickly pulling out the camera. *Click.*

"Michaela, and you are?" She took my leather and put it near the heater, shutting the door behind us.

I shook out my hair, and straightened my collar. "Lucky."

"Are you sure?" She smiled at me as she led me into the kitchen. Why does everyone go to the kitchen? Why isn't the kitchen called the living room, then? I followed and told the story of how my mom and dad met, having me nine months later to the day. I never did get another name. Lucky I am through and through. In theory.

Michaela sat us down and poured us both a glass of water and a shot of Jim Beam. I don't usually like liquor, but why be unsociable? I drank it down in one gulp and coughed for five minutes.

She wasn't as intimidating in her own home, surrounded by photographs and paintings. The counters held nothing; all was packed away out of sight, no dishes in the sink like at Christine's, no half-drunk coffee cups waiting to be cleaned up, and no piles of books on every surface imaginable. Michaela looked older, more my age, perhaps even in her forties, slight laughter lines around her eyes, a few streaks of gray, and a stillness that made me fall apart inside. I hid it well; I'd stopped coughing.

"Why don't you smoke in here? It's your place, right?" I noticed a large photograph of her and an older man, arm in arm. "Husband?" I asked.

"Brother. I share the house with him, John is his name, and he doesn't smoke, he has asthma, therefore I stand outside, smoke, and look around."

"Into the bathroom next door?"

Michaela grinned and tapped me on the arm. "Yes, and it was well worth it!"

I drank my water. Silently busy with the task of not spilling anything.

"Do you have any siblings?" she asked me. "Did your dad get lucky again and again?"

"Yeah, but not with my mom. I heard there's a sister in Arizona, but I've never met her." I was about to tell her more about how Dad was now, after the stroke, but then I got self-conscious. I shut up. I asked her a question instead. "Do you always invite strangers into your home like this?"

Her eyes, brown and deep, stared at mine for a while. No, not usually, she told me. There was something about me that drew her curiosity. "Here we are."

"Yes, here we are." I didn't know what to say after that. The moments ticked by. Then she stood and stretched her long lean frame, taking off the black fleece. She tucked the short red t-shirt into hip hugging jeans. I watched, and pulled out my camera. *Click.* She didn't hear. I sat back, realizing I'd been reaching toward her over the table. Oblivious of all else. With her back to me, Michaela turned on the tap, filled the kettle, and pulled out a couple of mugs and some tea bags. She turned on the radio. Classical FM. She looked me up and down again. "You need building up, by the looks of it. Peppermint and ginger sound all right? I'll add honey for energy. You'll need it."

I put the camera away.

10

"How was your day?" Christine asked, taking off the coat, scarf and hat, and putting the inevitably full bag of books on the floor beside her. The stereo played old school Led Zep. She sprawled across the sofa and stretched her legs into my lap. I'd made us another fire. I flinched a little at her touch but covered it by reaching for a log. I handed her my hot chocolate.

"Pretty full, considering." I told her about organizing the garage, meeting the neighbors and making Green Chile Stew for dinner. "All in a day's work!"

She drank and gave me the empty cup. "This is great—thanks, Lucky. Which neighbors did you meet? I know the old couple at the pink house near the main road, but the rest? There's a teacher or two in the area, I see them walking past fairly often. One of mine from school. But that's about it. Pretty transient around here, as you'd guess. People don't stick around much."

"One said she did."

"Really? Who?"

"She said she'd been here for five or more years, I think. Had been a student here in the '80s. She came back to teach. That was Michaela next door. Do you know her?"

"My professor? You met her?"

Luckily, Christine wasn't watching me so she missed seeing the heat creeping up my neck. "Er, yeah, I had tea with her."

"You didn't! Did you? That's crazy! She's my creative writing teacher at school. Tough woman. I'm intimidated by her, to be honest. What did you two talk about?"

Oh dear, her teacher? Yikes. That's a bit close to home. But, still, its not like anything was going on. Not really. Not with me and Chris.

I told her of how I'd read that the locals would be fined if they didn't clear their own parts of the sidewalks free of snow, even if it's the city plows that pile it up on them. It had struck me as rude somehow, to fine people like that. I'd gone in the garage to find gloves and shovels, which led to the whole reorganizing, or rather, organizing of tools and shelves. After that distraction, I'd headed out into the neighborhood and started to work. Knocking on doors, asking around as to who might need help, and yes, I'd met the Smiths at the Pink House. The old lady at the corner.

"She gave us those oatmeal cookies in that tin on the table. She's invited us both over for tea and cakes later this week. She referred to you as my 'nice young friend'!"

The fire spluttered and kicked out some ash onto the stone hearth. I leaned over and poked at the logs, then I swept the ash onto the paper and tipped it back in. I straightened the logs into a nice pile. "That's better," I said.

I heard Christine smother a laugh into a cough.

"What? What did I do?"

She shook her head and stood up, taking the empty mug with her. "I want cookies from your new Grandma. More hot choc, Lucky? And then you really do have to tell me about the Professor. What's she like? What's her home like? I've seen her out on the street but I've never been next door. Did she say anything about me?"

"Just asked how we knew each other."

"No! You didn't tell her—"

"What? That you picked me up at the diner? Oh, yes I did! She loved it. She wants you to write about it."

Christine threw me a look. And then a spoon. She missed me by a mile. With the spoon.

"Okay, I didn't really put it like that. But I did say we met yesterday and hit it off. Did you know she used to live in Ecuador? Teaching at some mountain village. Have you ever been there? She made it sound amazing. I almost want to drive down to Quito in Hilda."

"Hilda?"

"The Nissan. But then I looked at the map in your bedroom and saw it's a ridiculous distance. Coming up from the southwest was bad enough. Anyway, Michaela and I had a cup of tea and talked for a while about traveling. It was great. I like her."

Christine was watching me carefully. "Are you into her? But she's old!"

I laughed. "Do you know how old I am? Two years younger than her! Not even. One year and ten months, to be exact."

"Oh, really?" Christine arched her eyebrows. I grinned back at her not so subtle question, and explained that no, I'm not after Michaela, no more relationships for me. I didn't explain that there is still a lot of room to play, so to speak. Or that Michaela had already made the first offer. Or that from me came a counter-offer. I kept all that to myself.

Christine sat down again and we chatted about her schoolwork, that focus and passion of hers for living simply, knowing that America takes over fifty percent of the world's resources but has only a fraction of its population. Imbalanced, to say the least. We talked about Central and South America, how she'd love to go work there some day. Learn, teach, whatever it took to be a 'better person,' as she put it. Her drive impressed me, although I felt happy with the way things were; it suited me, to be honest.

Her laptop and books came out and off to homework-land went Chris while I heated up the stew. We didn't wait for Joanna this time. It remained just the two of us. I lay on the sofa and read. I took a photo of her frowning with pen raised to make a note.

Exhausted, I dozed off to the sound of her writing and the fire crackling softly to my left. I woke up when Chris tucked a thick wool blanket over me.

"Night, Lucky. Sleep well and no more nightmares, okay?"

She leaned over and kissed me gently on the lips, pausing a moment, looking into my eyes, but then stood upright and left me alone.

11

"I don't know how to do it, Mom. I don't know." I sat alone on a bench, looking out over the empty streets. Gray low-slung clouds hovered over me, echoing the way I felt. Some days I just missed my mom badly.

I shot the birds on the lamppost. With the camera. *Click.*

"There's this friend of mine, Christine, she's taken me in, letting me stay there, Mom, and I like her, but. Well, I don't know how to lighten up and just enjoy her. I don't know how to do this. Be nice. Be friendly. The other one, Michaela, she takes me as I am, and I'm not scared. It's simple. Not that there's anything going on, but, well. You know what I mean, right? I loved you, Mom, you know that, right? It's that I didn't like showing it. Felt weird. Awkward. Still do. I never did let you, oh, I don't know. At least, that's what Dad told me, that I was a difficult child, he said. Not easy. On anyone. Still not, I guess."

A few blackbirds talked back. The coffee in my hand had grown cold, but I sat on the wooden bench, smoking and breathing in the winter cold, watching over the town. I had a new black beanie with the Packers logo, one from the Salvation Army in this little student place. I liked it here, more my style than the city.

I'd driven Michaela's Toyota Prius last night, taking a few days away from it all. The Nissan was getting a new door. Now it was all about Me-Time. I'd needed Me-Time. Michaela got it, understood that being in the city was making me nuts, not sleeping again, and getting kind of crazy toward her, jealous, all because of that insomnia of mine. She didn't know why I didn't sleep so good, or that I'd left my dad at the hospital and just disappeared. The hospital couldn't get a hold of me, and couldn't do anything until they did. Later, I'd deal with it later.

Michaela gave me the keys to the car and told me to come back in a better mood. Christine hardly noticed me these days, too busy with some thesis. I'd left her a note, saying I'd be back over the weekend.

Steven's Point offered me a Bed and Breakfast in the downtown area, overlooking the few local businesses still open in winter. The tourists that make the town numbers swell in summer had fallen away and left only the hardiest students. Perfect for me after coming from Santa Fe, which also has tons of tourists come and go, feeding the pockets of the galleries and the restaurants. I understood this calmer time of the year. I liked it. A city as big as Madison had begun to overwhelm me, but Steven's Point struck me as much less claustrophobic. More my pace. My style. I wouldn't get beaten up somewhere like here, would I? Nope, it felt pretty safe to be me.

I pulled out the camera, cleaned the lens and scrolled through the last few weeks. Memories. Images. Conversations. Tastes. All came back to me. I erased those that just didn't work for me, the ones that I deemed boring in compilation, and all those I'd taken with a standard eye to camera shot. Not interesting enough to keep. The ones I shot from the hip caught my attention. Chris at the diner, that first morning, as she sat alone waiting for me to finish my meal. Joanna in her apron and tucking a stray hair while talking to a family about the pancakes. Christine bent over her books at the kitchen table. The snow shovels' view of the city plow. Looking down at my own boots, waiting for Michaela to let me in to her place, and a few of the walk down her hallway. The table top, with two mugs, and a bottle of Jim Beam. Michaela's hips. My boots left lying by her woodstove. The last one was of Christine on the swing, head thrown back, as we played one afternoon at the park next to Lake Mendota.

I walked back to the car up the main street and let myself in. I wanted more. More what, I didn't know. I sipped the coffee and put the Sony back in my jacket, within easy reach. I started the engine and just drove. No destination. No adrenalin. Driving for the sake of it, not to escape. The snow had melted for a day or two and I'd read that we had a few weeks till it really would settle. I had a week then, to decide. Do I stay? Go? If I go, where to? North? I'd freeze unless I got that window replaced. If I stayed, well, do I stay with Christine? Do I keep seeing Michaela in the mornings? How do I get them both?

I finally stopped driving in Custer, a small town nearby, empty roads, small wooden homes, a post office and three bars of note. The Pit Stop, Clancy's Stone Lion and the one I chose, No Problem. I let myself in to find it almost empty but for few old geezers. They stopped talking and turned to me. Friendly like. But still, a little unnerving.

"Can I get you something?"

"Yes, I'd like something warming. A Jim Beam, if you have it?" I'd developed a taste for the stuff.

"Not from around here?" The bartender ambled back to pour me a shot. His white hair and beard needed a trim, but his hands were clean and his smile wide. I fingered the camera and put it on the counter in front of me, fiddling with it unthinkingly. The bartender took my five dollars and turned to get the change. *Click.* I snapped away, focusing along and past the glass to the couple at the end of the bar, smokes in hand, laughing at the sitcom on television set above them. I drank my shot and asked for another. "Just visiting," I told him. "Not sure where to next. Any suggestions?"

"Well, if you like the snow, stay here. If you like the heat, get out now while you can!" He cackled loudly. "Right, Daniel? Get out if you can?"

Daniel swiveled and nodded seriously. "I'd leave if I was you. Too hard, unless you got family here. Do you?"

I shook my head. No, I told them, alone these days.

"That's sad. Where are your folks?"

"Mom died when I was a kid. Dad, well, he had a stroke a few months ago."

"In Madison? That's too bad; I bet it's a real shame to see him like that. I lost my parents ten years ago, and I still think of them." Daniel offered me a Marlboro. I took it and lit the one in his hand at the same time. He was wrinkled, tanned by too many years on the farm. He wore a thick carhardt jacket even with the fire raging only five feet way. I sweated and fidgeted. I wanted to say, *but you're old. I'm only 38, too young to be alone.* I held it back. Like I had with Michaela. And Chris. Neither knew much about me. I drank more Jim Beam. It warmed my toes, that's my excuse. Plus I had nowhere else to go.

"He's in New Mexico."

"Mexico? That's an awful long way. What's he doing there? And why aren't you with him?" Dave sat back to stare briefly at the television. Apparently I was more interesting.

"Mexico, huh."

I explained that I meant Santa Fe, New Mexico, some sixteen hundred miles from here, more or less. I needed to get away, we'd never been close, not since I was a teenager and went away. I didn't talk about the homes Dad sent me to, hoping they'd straighten me out. Stop the thieving and vandalism. And it worked. It cost us, though. "We don't get along," is all I said. "He can't hear me, anyway. Can't speak any more. He just sort of lies there." I shook away the images in my head, and leaned back, the camera took another few shots of the bar top, and of my growing collection of glasses and cigarette butts. No longer that dark or cold in here, I stared at the sign, No Problem, and I smiled. Yep, this was what I'd needed.

Another shot appeared. And another.

Daniel turned to his friends and me both. "I reckon it's a sad day when the dad's in the hospital alone, and the kid's miles away. Bad luck to you both. Not what I want for myself. You think about that, Dave? Being alone like that?"

"I wonder if he can hear? Don't they say that the hearing is the last sense to leave?" His friend Dave shook his head, thinking hard. I listened to them discussing comas and stroke victims. I didn't want to talk about it. But I did. Tried to tell them why I was in Wisconsin. Why seeing him like that in the hospital broke me, it just destroyed me. I spent the afternoon talking more to Dave and Daniel than I had with either Chris or Michaela. I told them everything.

Some time later that night, Daniel walked me back to his place, a few doors away. I fell onto the couch next to the woodstove, not even taking my boots off. Exhausted and drunk into silence, I listened as Daniel sat up for hours telling me about the area, his family's struggles in the Great Depression, the three tours in Vietnam, and his own kids now living in Michigan; the details became part of my dreams. It was an old farmhouse, dating back to when all this land was cattle and crops. It wasn't connected to any of the Steven's Point suburbs until recently, he said. He'd grown up here in Custer, learned all about migration and over-population first hand.

I wanted to bring Chris to talk to him about her theories. I don't remember much else.

12

I took a couple of days to myself, staying with Daniel, chopping wood for him as a thank you. I bucked two huge piles and stacked them near the back door. His smile was worth every aching bone. We celebrated by making a fire to heat the whole home and cooked cowboy coffee on top. I made up some stew, New Mexican style, and lots of chiles, potatoes and whatever else I found in his kitchen. We hunkered down in front of the flames and ate in silence.

"Are you going to visit your dad?"

"I don't know. I should. Maybe later. I want to. But. I don't know."

He ate some more and leaned back to light a smoke. "It's now or never, you know that, right? Family. We don't know when they'll be gone. But I can tell you this, Lucky, once he's gone, you'll ache. Deep, so deeply that no one can touch it. No one can help you then. It changes a person." He stood up and left the room and I heard him head up the stairs.

I pulled out my phone. No messages. No texts. I sent another to Michaela, a flirtatious little note to make her smile. I missed playing with her. I wanted to fall into bed with her and make her laugh at my antics. Was she thinking about me? I called. No answer. I left a message at her house. I knew she'd asked me not to, something about keeping us separate from her brother John, but I wanted to hear from her. I didn't know why. I'd nearly told the answer machine about the photos I'd taken of her sleeping, and how once I'd printed them up, the detail of her skin and the relaxation around her eyes was breathtaking. I caught myself, though, and hung up quickly.

But I'd shown Daniel the prints and he'd sighed in remembrance of his own lovers now come and gone. He'd passed the photos back and nodded. Again, he said nothing more.

I pulled out some other prints and shuffled them on the low table next to me. Christine. Michaela. Do I stay? Who do I stay with? I missed the expanse of the southwest. These unending rolling hills, lakes and trees delighted some part of me, but mostly overwhelmed me, tightened my chest, and fought hard with my sense of beauty. It didn't inspire my need to take shots. The camera lay unused in my pocket. Only the people I'd met drew me. Landscapes here suffocated me. But the people distracted me nicely. Very nicely.

Daniel came back downstairs with a box in his hands. He lay it down in front of me and took the lid off. Old black and white photos packed it to the brim.

"It took a while to find this old shoebox, but I knew I had it. There's my mom. Beautiful, isn't she? Black hair in a tight bun, smelling of cooking and woodstoves, that's what I remember most about her. This here's my sister, Jane, plain Jane, but she hated that name. She died in her teens, one bad winter, before the doctor moved nearby. Pneumonia. This is Dad here, this tall skinny one in the back with the black hair and beard, he lasted a long, long time. In fact, you'd have met him if you'd been here last year. He made it till last Thanksgiving. Almost a hundred. Funny how people die around the holidays, isn't it?"

I hardly listened. The photos captivated me. And shamed me. All these memories shut away in a box, upstairs, never shown or enjoyed. Why then did I do the same? Why take all these shots only to keep them for my eyes alone?

Daniel kept talking, on a roll, all about life in Wisconsin, the winter ice fishing that almost cost him his life when he was a foolhardy kid. The cabin up north where the boys would go hunting. The lakes everywhere, and how he'd taken his first girlfriend skinny-dipping. They'd been married within six months and a kid on the way. I watched him holding the pictures. I watched the reverence in his touch, in his eyes, now moist at the stories he told, and my heart broke open. My hands shook. I blinked rapidly. I had no words for it. Something magical broke free in me.

Click.

After Daniel took the box back upstairs with him, I tried calling Michaela again. I started to leave a message when she picked up.

"Yes, Lucky?"

"Hey! I didn't think I'd find you in. How are you? I've missed you! Can I come back tomorrow? Do you have classes in the afternoon?"

There was a slight pause. "Yes, I have a double at noon. I'll be home after that."

I rushed on, starting to describe Daniel and his memories and what have you when she cut me off.

"Look, you can tell me tomorrow. I have company right now."

"Oh."

"I'll see you tomorrow afternoon. Have a nice drive home, Lucky. I'll see you tomorrow."

"Oh."

She hung up.

I sat there with the phone on my lap. Company? Who? Was she seeing someone? I almost called her back. But I knew better. I put the phone in my pocket. Who's over there? She didn't say she missed me. I pulled out the prints of her in bed. The hairs on her forearm backlit. Her left thigh relaxed and half covered by the wool blanket, inviting my touch. The curve under her breast, a slight touch of sweat, a few hours later. Her hand reaching toward the camera, reaching for me, again.

I remembered that first time asking if I could take shots of her. She'd thought I was crazy. Admittedly, I'd already taken some in the kitchen, but I'd held out the camera to her, showing how small and inconsequential it looked. She still thought I was incredibly crazy. I'd only been talking to her at that point for an hour, at most. But she grinned. She told me I could take photos if we were alone, but never in public. I asked then if she'd undress for me.

She'd held out her hand, and I clicked. She laughed. I followed her upstairs and to the bedroom to the right. She opened the door, led me inside, and sat me down. You're not to move, she instructed me, you're not to touch me, and those are the only rules for now. Agreed?

Agreed.

I texted Michaela a note to say I had photos for her. I'd bring them by. I didn't hear back from her. I no longer wanted to keep these images in my camera or in my head, for me alone. What that meant, I didn't know. The photos had a life of their own. I couldn't hide them any more. That was all I knew.

No reply from Michaela. Is she too busy with her 'company'? I stared at the phone. Call me back, dammit. She didn't.

I called Christine.

"LUCKY!"

I almost dropped the phone. Chris started to babble away, full of questions and worries and laughter at hearing my voice. "Come home!" she urged. "I've missed having you cook for me, for us!" I heard Joanna laughing with her in the kitchen. I heard pans clattering and a few choice words in the background. "She's trying to make a soup. It's not going so well. And we've run out of those cookies! We need you here! Where are you? What you doing and why?"

We chatted for ages, and then set it that I'd see her for supper that next night; they both had classes till seven, and would be home shortly afterwards.

"You still have keys, right?"

I grinned into the phone. "Yeah, I do, thanks, Chris. I'll bring you something from Custer, I promise."

"Oh, Lucky. I'd like that."

What to bring her? Why did I have to offer? Crap at buying presents, I had to find something. I'd look in the morning. For the rest of the night, though, I looked at the prints of my lover. I held them close, judged some as being technically good, but I hadn't captured the energy I'd wanted. The sensuality I knew so intimately. All but one was lacking. Her hand reaching for me, that one grabbed at me each time. A keeper. I'd keep that one. I'd try to keep Michaela, too.

13

The last time I saw Mike was at the Cowgirl. We'd gone to talk. He'd asked me to. Said we were family, that we should talk.

I listened. He talked and talked and talked. It didn't mean shit to me. Just words. Words to explain his selfish crap, his actions, fucking my girlfriend. How reasonable he thought he was. I drank my beer, on his tab. I looked around at all the television screens and half watched the Saints cream the Cowboys. Boring, it was too easy for the Saints. I didn't want to make it too easy for Mike. I looked over at him, saw his mouth moving, but the words didn't make sense to me.

I interrupted him. "When your dad has had a stroke and is in a coma, Mike, and when your best friend fucks your girlfriend behind your back at the same time, and then your dog gets lost in the hills, well, then we can talk. Later. " I decked him. With one punch, he fell to the floor.

Beer glasses flew. Stools falling. Locals jumping in. Bouncers yelling. TV blaring in the background. Blood soaking me. I kicked him once more. Hard. Ferocious. He smashed back against the bar. He stopped moving. He fell silent. And then he screamed.

I ran. I ran home. I packed my bags. I threw out Susan's stuff onto Manhattan Street with a 'Free' sign and threw everything into the Nissan. I took a photo. The rusted yellow four by four truck with a huge pile of bedding and bags tossed inside. *Click.* I left. I left my home. My life in Santa Fe. I drove as far as I could. I made it to Las Vegas. Las Vegas, New Mexico, that is.

14

I drove Michaela's car into town and parked near the school. Walking down State Street, past the University Bookstore with all the Bucky Badger merchandise and a few college books, and then through the mall and toward Monona Terrace. I spotted Christine by the fountain but I kept on walking. I needed to return the keys to Michaela. I wanted to. I wanted to see her.

I found her outside, at a metal patio table near the lake, with the sailing boats, sunshine and blue sky highlighting her silhouette and drawing me to her, like a moth. About to be burned.

"Hey, there, Michaela! Here are your keys; thanks for letting me use your car. It was amazing to get out of town for a few days. I can't wait to tell you about Daniel and his pictures." I looked around the table. Everybody stared at me curiously. "I'm Lucky," I told them.

"So I hear," said the older man to her right, his arm draped behind Michaela, and with a sly smile he looked me up and down. The other three chuckled. Did you know people really could chuckle? It was eerie.

I glanced back at Michaela. She stared at me impassively but didn't introduce me, saying only, "Thanks, Lucky. I was expecting to see you later."

"Well, yes, I just was…" I didn't finish. Her eyes told me not to. I walked away, dropping the keys on the guy's lap, while staring at her. "Thanks a lot. Bye."

In the foyer, I bumped into Christine on her way to swim at the gym. Want to come? she asked. I shrugged and kept walking past all the students, the backpacks and the bikes. I wanted to curl up. Alone. Chris followed me.

"What's wrong? What happened?" she followed me and grabbed my arm when I ignored her. I turned suddenly and she ran into me, laughing. But I wasn't. And then she wasn't either. "Are you okay, Lucky? You look like you saw a ghost."

I couldn't look her in the eyes. I looked at my boots instead.

"Nothing, rough morning. I'm tired. I want to go back to your place, lie around, if that's okay."

"Of course." She touched my cheek lightly. "I'll see you this afternoon." She walked away, catching up with a gaggle of her friends. I took out the camera and caught her shadow running to keep up.

I headed back to the terrace and ordered a beer and a shot. I sat near the door, with my back to the school, and zoomed in on Michaela's friends. *Click.* I took five photographs. I stared until I could take it no more.

I pulled out my other jeans from the laundry bag, riffled through and found the shorts and tees and couple pairs of socks. The bathroom closed in on me. I sat on the edge of the tub, and stared at the green walls, trying to slow down. I took another deep breath, one after another. I pulled my toothbrush from the cup on the sink. I put that in the backpack with the rest of my stuff. What else? Anything?

I left the towel. It didn't mean anything to me, just bought it the other week on Willy Street. My hands shook but I took out the camera anyway. *Click.*

I cleaned up. And I left.

I drove through town and onto the main highway south. Heading south toward Iowa again. Toward those oh-so-friendly idiots in the big truck. I drove down the wide hectic multi-lane streets, with malls on both sides of me, gas stations; this was a side of Madison I didn't know. I froze. In more ways than one. I wished the heater hadn't broken last week.

I stopped at the first Denny's I saw and pulled up. I stared through the windows into the plastic coated idea of 'family' dining. I couldn't do it. I drove back to the school downtown. I parked on Frat row, outside some huge mansion and walked back to the Terrace. The foyer was empty but there were a few people passing by. The bar was closed. The bookshop sat quiet. I looked out to the lakeside cafe, to the tables sitting unused in the late afternoon sun. Michaela had gone.

Christine had gone. And I wanted to be gone, too. But I couldn't do it. I drove back to Chris's home and let myself in. I put my laundry back in the machine and ran a bath. I closed the curtains.

"Hi." Christine came up to me and gave a quick peck on the cheek before dropping her bag on the floor beside me. She sat down.

She didn't ask but I could see the question in her eyes. How was I? Not so good. Clean but not so good. I'd spent an hour or so in the tub, soaking, trying to calm down and settle in to being here again. I'd wanted to leave, drive off. It's what I knew best. It's what I usually did. That is, until Susan. She tamed me, she made me more housebroken and settled than anyone else, my parents included. That's what she changed about me, from constant movement to staying home.

But she left me, left me for Mike. Not the bloody Alpacas, not an animal, just my best friend. When did they get together? It's not like I'd had regular work hours. Nor a job to take me away from home that much. Don't tell me it was her overtime? At work at the radio station? Fuck 'em both. I turned to Christine. "Mike called me today. This afternoon, out of the blue."

"Your friend from Santa Fe?"

I nodded. "Yep. He took my girlfriend from me. I haven't talked to him in ages." I hadn't told Christine much, just the basics. Who was who, that type of thing. The basics. Not the more gruesome aftermath of our last conversation. "I'd been lying in the tub when the phone rang. I climbed out to get it and saw it was Mike. I couldn't decide what to do. So I left it. Would you listen to his message?"

"You didn't listen to it? When did he call?"

"About two hours ago. Will you?"

She took the phone that I held out. "What's your code?"

I told her. I put another log on the fire. Chris had told me last week how she and Joanna never bothered with it, used the forced air heat system instead. I'd laughed. The next day I found someone selling wood by the truckload and got it delivered. Well worth it. I tried not to listen to the voice on the phone. I couldn't help it, though.

Chris held it out. "It's fine. He asks how you are. Says hello. Not much more than that. Says he's seen your dad a few times. Oh, and he says he's been looking for Blue, but had no luck so far. Want to listen?"

I shook my head. I leaned back against the green sofa and closed my eyes. I saw my room in Santa Fe, the one I'd shared with Susan. It had been gold and green; the plaster had been painted brightly years before we'd moved in together, faded by the time we moved in. I liked it so much that we kept it as it was. The wooden floors were scuffed and well worn. The bedroom sat at the back of the house, facing Agua Fria Street and the huge yard with the two ancient apricot and apple trees that gave my gentle dog the shade she'd needed in the height of summer. My girl. Blue. Sweet Blue. I missed her. I didn't even want to think about her lost in the mountains, but it came back to me. How we'd gone for a walk up in the Sangre de Christo hills, hiking the day after I'd found Susan gone.

We'd walked. She ran. My Border Collie mutt ran and ran and ran. I heard her yelping in glee as she found a rabbit or something, her voice getting more and more distant. I heard her. I called. I yelled and screamed. She didn't come back.

I'd run and screamed and waited for hours, staying the night in my truck, coming and going to that very trail every day. For a week or more. Until I left town. I left her alone in the hills.

I sat back on the couch and closed my eyes, holding it all in. Chris stroked my hair and I leaned into her touch. I kept my eyes closed and thought of all I'd left. All I'd lost. Pathetic. I was pathetic, I knew it.

Chris stroked my hair. My cheek. Eyes. Mouth. I reached for her blindly. Needing her. My eyes half-opened when I first kissed her. Pulled her in. Kept her close. And she pulled me in deeper.

15

I ran along the lakefront, tiring myself as much as I could. I'd woken with Christine curled up next to me, a smug little smile on her lips. I'd watched her dream. I took my camera out. One. Just one, I promised myself. *Click.*

I crept out of bed and threw on my clothes. If Blue was with me, I'd have a reason to leave. I did it anyway. I left no note, only the present, that packet I'd brought back from Custer, all about the Green Sustainable festival they put on each year. I'd included a photo of Daniel on his porch. I wanted to tell her all about him, about the ideas I'd had for my photographs.

Later. I'd tell her later. She didn't know yet that I'd decided to take it further, photography. It was a need for me to take photos. I made sense of the world through these images. It was time to show these images, show what I make of life, and it was time to tell the stories I knew.

I ran up Willy Street, took the first left and jogged to the water's edge. Two blocks and then right again, with the sun coming up over the far side of Lake Mendota. I ran until the stitch in my side knocked me down. Who was I kidding? I'm not a runner, never have been.

I came up to the beach with the kid's park. I sat on a swing and lit a smoke. What had I done now? Sex. Sex always messes things up. I took out the camera again and set the self-timer, and stood with the sun behind me. A mess. Yep, a mess of a morning. Now what? Take photos, that's what. All around I saw the signs of approaching winter. The leaves dried and golden lay in scattered piles on the grass. The beach hut was locked. The trashcans were turned upside down. No sign of life that day. The park lay empty as I prowled around the perimeter. *Click.*

A cop car pulled up. "Can I help you?"

I walked up and explained I was from New Mexico, visiting friends, taking photos, nothing sinister. He didn't ask for my I.D. I was worried that Mike had pressed charges against me. He wouldn't, would he? Nah.

The cop left. I stayed. Took photos of my boots against the water's edge. Beautiful. Crisp light, a cloudless sky, bright blue water and my dirt brown work boots. I lay on the sand and dreamed of meeting Susan. I dreamed of Blue as a puppy. I dreamed of happier days.

I woke to the cold wind cutting me deep. I woke up to find the camera clutched in my hands, next to my heart. What to do with these photos?

On State Street, I walked into the first gallery I came across. One of the only ones. I asked to talk to the manager. A middle-aged balding man in a gray corduroy coat and blue tie walked up to me with a wide smile.

"Can I help you?"

I pulled out my camera.

James Laughlin was not only the manager but also an avid photographer himself. He took my camera and looked it over. He looked me over. "Ah, yes, I see," he said. "These Cybershots have become one of the best small digitals around. High resolution. 14 MB. Fits in any pocket. Great for amateurs." I bristled. "And professionals alike," he added. "Yes, I can see why you use this. Good choice. Now, let's see what you've done with it, shall we?"

I followed him past the high metal and glass table at the front door, glancing briefly at the huge oil landscapes, a couple of sculptures on pedestals, a few portraits on the back wall, and into a brightly lit office. He sat down and waved me to come behind the desk to join him. I stood slightly to his right, and looked over his shoulder. On the table were a laptop and an empty mug. He turned my camera on, reaching for his reading glasses, and he began to scroll through the memory. I started to explain but he cut me off, saying that the photos needed to stand alone, without words.

I stood there in my clean black jeans and the thick wool sweater that I'd borrowed from Chris's pile of winter wear. I pushed my hair back out of my eyes—I needed to cut it again soon, it was getting too scruffy and falling onto my nose at odd times. My nails needed a trim. Funny, the things I noticed as I stood waiting.

James sat in his big brown leather chair and kept looking, making little noises of approval. He started from the beginning again, still not talking to me directly. I looked around the office, with the tall window looking out on to a main side street; the locals and students out there walking past were oblivious of how nerve wracking a day this was. The office buildings opposite stood tall and new, with a sense of high-end clientele. Was that good for business? The art world? It was nothing I knew about.

I looked around the office again. The white carpet had been vacuumed and still had the stripes leading back to the main gallery room. I heard chatting outside, and the door opening and closing. The radio came on with subtle classical strings, a soothing distraction. I listened, trying to recognize what was playing. I only really know reggae, not the kind for background music you'd want to sell expensive paintings, now is it? James scratched his chin, and reached for the laptop. A Mac. I have a Mac, I thought. But smaller.

"You have a good eye for composition, Lucky. Very interesting. Now, let's see how they look enlarged, shall we? See if the focus and detail stands up to scrutiny?" He smiled and took the memory stick and plugged it in. I watched silently, not much to say.

James called out to his helper in the front, asking for a pot of coffee for us both, turning to me saying we might as well be comfortable and satiated. He had a feeling he could look at these images for a long time coming.

"No more interviews today, Jen, okay? I'm busy with a new photographer. This is Lucky, and this is an example of a Lucky Shot."

An image came up of Michaela's hand reaching for me, her bronze golden skin touched by candlelight, the moisture on her wrist, the blurred hint of a bed behind. Jen sighed and leaned in close.

"Exactly." James sat back in satisfaction. "That is the reaction we want, and this is what we'll be getting from you, Lucky." He put his hand in mine and held on, staring at me solidly while Jen stared at the image on the screen.

I looked back and forth between them both. Jen stood back up, and smiled, saying, "Very, very nice. Thank you." She left with a nod to her boss. They shared some look as she walked out, closing the big wooden door behind her.

James turned back and poured us both coffee. He focused again on the screen and took out a pen and paper from the top drawer, and he started to make notes.

I drank the coffee and watched more closely, wondering what it was he saw in some of the images, why some struck him enough to make a mark worth remembering? He didn't explain, simply flicked back and forth through the two hundred photos I'd kept since leaving Santa Fe.

"Do you have more? Or is this a recent hobby?"

"Lifelong, I've always taken photos. I even worked at a studio for while. I had a Canon FT for ages, then a cheap digital. This one is new to me, I've only had it for the last couple of years, at the most. I printed a handful of these new photos up the other day. I have them back at the house I'm staying at. I have more on my computer, from when I lived in New Mexico." Babbling nervously, I couldn't help it.

"I'd like to see the prints you made."

"If you don't mind me asking, why? You have everything new here." I pointed to his screen.

James sipped his now cold coffee and said he was interested in understanding what I found compelling, what had I wanted to see in more detail. Apparently it would tell him a lot as to whether this was fluke, instinct, or something else. I could have told him that. It was a need, nothing more.

"I'd like to see them," he repeated. "Tomorrow, if you can. I'll also need you to bring releases from your models. Have you ever shown your work here? Or anywhere?"

I shook my head. "Never thought of it until just now. Why?"

"We'll need an artist's statement, too. Something for us to print up for the media, and to go with your photographs when we show them here."

"A show?"

"Didn't you think I was serious about the response to your work? It's engaging on many levels, Lucky. It's sensual, erotic and the emotionality of each piece is striking in a deeply moving manner. I want us to talk more tomorrow. Let's make a plan for you to return tomorrow in time for a business lunch with John, the owner. We refer to ourselves as the three Jays. Can you make it?" I nodded. He continued. "I'll keep these images, save them if you trust me. Do you?"

I nodded again and thrust my hand at him like a teenager on a dare. James laughed and we shook a deal. A gentlemen's handshake was good enough for me.

I left with the camera, sneaking a couple of shots from my hip of James at his desk, staring again at the computer in front of him, one of the door open for me, the entrance to the gallery with Jen sunning herself as she looked up the street toward the Capitol building.

16

"You what? You did *what?*"

Christine and Joanna stood slack-jawed, both stunned by my sudden and rather unusual news. I held out the camera. Half-scared they'd yell at me for taking photos without asking. Half-thrilled to make them shriek. I told them again.

"I went to the Stone gallery on State Street and James, the manager, he loved my work, my body of work, and wants to show my photos, help me get professionally recognized in town. Can you believe it?"

Hell no, was the reply, but they tickled and punched and laughed with me. Incredibly excited. Christine threw her arms around me and gave me the tightest hug I'd had in ages. She kissed me smartly on the mouth and pulled away, eyes bright and delighted.

Joanna giggled. "Like that, huh? When did that happen? I've been working too much." She punched me lightly, shaking her head in mock disapproval. Chris laughed out loud again and took the camera from me. I grabbed it back.

"No. Wait. Let me. I have some printed out to show you both. I'll get them for you." I took the camera and put it in my pocket.

I found the prints I'd made in Custer with Daniel. I spread some of them out on the table, moving Joanna's bag onto a seat. The light was good, full overhead and the images sat clearly before them. I stood back and watched their faces. I kept aside the prints of Michaela.

Chris still wore her pajamas from that morning, a mix of a pink soft cotton top and men's pants, striped blue and green. She glanced up at me and caught me looking, blushed and turned her attention back to the photographs. Joanna held up the one of Christine on the swing, that first time at the park together. She raised an eyebrow.

"How long has this been going on? Where did you go? Why wasn't I there?" She put it on the table again and asked for the details, saying she hadn't seen Chris that relaxed or silly in months.

"Months?"

They both glanced at the other. Chris shrugged and sat down with her back to the fire.

"Yep. I tried dating a friend, we laughed a lot, but that was about it. Not much else happened. A quick fumble one night and then…well, you can guess!" She didn't quite look at me.

"Ah, yes, friends. But you had fun, right?"

Joanna watched us both carefully. But then Chris and I caught each other's eyes and we both laughed and the tension dropped. "Yeah, we did."

"I know the feeling." I held my hands out, empty. "Well, anyway, enough about you!" I joked. "Back to me, I have to write an artist's statement to take with me tomorrow. What the hell does that mean? What do I do?" I sat next to Chris and looked up at Joanna, saying, "Help!"

"Well, let's see. How about we get some food together, look at the photos you're taking back and we'll work out why you do what you do. That's about it, right?" Joanna brushed a stray hair out of her eyes and stood up. "Food first. I'll cook."

For the rest of the evening, I kept the camera out of reach of wandering hands and eyes. I needed to decide what to do with the photos of Michaela.

I needed to talk to her. I sent her a short text but heard nothing back. I tried calling, but didn't leave a message. I wanted to tell her all about the gallery and Daniel and my hopes. She'd get it.

We'd had some great conversations across her kitchen table. Full of stories of her various creative ideas and what she's done with her artwork, how she writes and paints and makes stuff with found objects. A well-rounded artist. I'd been envious of her. Now I wanted to tell her my news. I sent another text. Short, light, trying to be teasing, I hoped she'd get back to me. She didn't.

I joined the kitchen crew. Chris had subtly taken over, with Joanna chopping the veggies and Chris making a stir-fry with chicken. It smelled amazing. I put on the brown rice. I talked of how I'd been taking photos the whole trip, just as a way to keep a record of all I felt and saw on my way. It helped me stay connected, not disappear into my head too much. James had seen most of them, liked the 'emotionality' of them.

"Is that a word?" Joanna looked up from the garlic and onions.

"I don't think so, but I didn't want to correct him. Anyway, it was the feelings that the pictures stirred up that intrigued him. I have to try to explain tomorrow what I meant by them. But it isn't so simple. I take them. I look at them. Now I want to share them."

Joanna nodded. "That sounds pretty simple to me. Tell them how it just came to you after meeting Daniel, after seeing his box of old black and whites, that you wanted yours to live on, beyond your own eyes and memories. Do you want to show them? Are you ready to be asked about them all?"

"All?"

She nodded. "I imagine that the gallery will want to put together a solid show. That's the reputation of the place, high publicity, interviews, and openings, all of it. You'll have to meet and greet everyone, Lucky. They'll ask you all about yourself. And the photos, of course. The stories behind them."

I didn't like the sound of that. I still had images that I wasn't sure I could show anyone. Chris didn't know about Michaela and me. That was my main concern. How to tell her? Or did I have to? Maybe not. Maybe I could keep those photos vague, no name put next to them. I still had to work out how to get the releases, though. That'd be tricky.

My phone vibrated and I glanced down. It was Michaela calling me. I pressed the silence button on the side. I'd get that later. In a few minutes, I'd go out for a smoke. I'd listen to the message, maybe even pop next door to see her, when the cooking took all their attention. No one would miss me.

I knocked on the door and waited. Outside the temperature had dropped rapidly and in the dark winter evening, I shivered. I stood with camera in hand, not wanting to chicken out. The back door opened up and a man I recognized from his photograph stood there. John. The brother I hadn't met. He smiled uncertainly, asking, "Can I help you?"

"Hi. I'm looking for Michaela. Is she home?" and I held out my hand to him. He shook it but didn't invite me in. He looked interested but also confused. He stood as tall as Michaela, with similar dark hair; his was short and slicked back, and with a touch of salt and pepper. The suit he wore was a deep stormy gray, with a soft pink shirt and black tie. Quite formal.

I stood there in my clean jeans, black sweatshirt and a blue beanie.

He told me, "We have company tonight—could you come back tomorrow instead? She'll be home in the morning. I have a meeting at lunchtime but Mickey will be around. All right?" He didn't really give me time to answer but turned away from me into the kitchen.

I smelled roast beef, of all things, and thought of my mom. He glanced back while pushing the door closed on me, saying "See you tomorrow."

Click.

Christine passed me a glass of red wine with a questioning look. I said nothing. She headed back to the kitchen, saying I had ten minutes or so. I nodded and drank a huge gulp and tried to head off the start of another shitty mood. I shook myself and sat at the table, taking out a pen and paper from my bag. I hooked up the laptop and downloaded the most recent photos I'd taken and saved. I started to edit them, rotate, name, crop and even occasionally delete.

I went through them, one by one. How was I supposed to get releases? I had no idea. I closed the computer with a sigh. I wrote the beginnings of the statement.

"I slept until ten or so, I think—what a relaxing day this has been. Just home with the books and food in the fridge!" Christine smiled as she finished off her wine.

Joanna leaned back in her chair. "I like this, the formal dinner at the table. It's been a while, hasn't it?" She stood up and cleaned off the plates. "Tea or coffee? More wine? What do you think, Chris? A night off for once? No books at all?"

We'd spread out across the table, with plates, dishes, empty glasses, wine bottles and even a bowl of fruit and cheeses. Quite the meal. I licked my spoon again. I was incredibly full and relaxed.

My phone buzzed. Michaela. I silenced it again. I didn't want to talk to her. Joanna told me to go ahead and take it if I wanted, no problem. I shook my head and poured another round of wine for each of us. Chris had put on *Such a Strong Persuader* by Robert Cray, and it lent itself to the mood I was in. Too aware of both Chris and

Michaela and the mess I'd got myself in. I drank some more and went out for another smoke.

Chris joined me and crawled under my jacket. "Are you okay, Lucky? Is this okay?"

"Yeah, pretty good. I'm tired, though. Aren't you?"

"No, like I said, I stayed home today, still in my pajamas. I cleaned the kitchen, did laundry, cooked some soup and read my books. It's been a perfect day. Couple of days." She peeked a glance up at me, and I smiled, giving her a quick kiss on the forehead. Not very romantic, I know, but I had other things on my mind.

"Sorry, I'm a bit distracted. A lot to think about. I'm not sure how to do this show, whether I stay or go." Chris froze next to me, not moving, just listening as I talked out loud to myself. Working it out. "Do I stay? What do I do? Where? Here? But it was only supposed to be a few days, you know?"

"Don't you like it with us? With me?" Her voice shook slightly. She held on under the coat. She reached for my camera and I laughingly, worriedly, got her to look at me. I kissed her. Deeply. Her hands stopped their wanderings and she hugged me to her. The ice storm we'd been expecting was heading into town in the next day or two and you could tell: The night froze each breath between us, making huge clouds whenever we spoke out loud.

We stayed out there, though, keeping each other warm and chatting quietly about the gallery, the trip back to New Mexico, and when I'd go if I did. "I don't know, Chris," I said. "Not really sure of what I'm doing. New Mexico—I have things I need to take care of there. I can't make up my mind, though. Later, I'll work it out later. Does it bother you? That I might be going soon? It's nothing personal."

"That's the phrase that doesn't work for me," she said, "And anyway, I hadn't been looking for more. Still unsure of you, to be honest. You're holding something back and I don't know what." She stood back and looked at me wonderingly.

I put the smoke out. "Let's go back inside. Joanna will be waiting for us." I held out my hand and walked her ahead of me. The door across the way opened and Michaela headed out with a cigarette already lit. I didn't look back.

17

I walked into the gallery with the laptop, my notes, and a handful of prints. I'd tossed away my coffee cup a block away. The last cigarette stubbed out at two hundred feet. I sucked a mint. I smoothed back my hair. I'd ended up cutting it last night with Christine's help in the bathroom. We'd had a shower together, and then a distracted hair cut, with Chris laughing the whole time, rubbing my shoulders and sitting me in the claw-foot tub as she took care of me.

Michaela watched us from her porch through the windows until I'd closed the curtains. I'd turned down the lights, lit the candle and forgot the rest of the world. Michaela, that is.

Jen greeted me at the gallery door with a warm smile and introduced me to someone, a customer, as their newest photographer.

"Oh, really? You must show me some of your work. I *love* to see emerging artists." The lady held out her hand to me and passed me her business card. I put it in my jacket pocket before I lost it. "Where are you from? I haven't heard of a new artist here. Jen? Tell me more!" She held onto my hand as Jen told her how I'd walked in the day before.

"John's expecting Lucky to be on time. You might want to let go now!" Jen teased the client before waving me back to the office with a smile.

I knocked on the door. I waited until I heard the answering welcome. I walked inside, ready to meet the boss. John stood up. John. Michaela's brother. He stared at me and then turned to James with an eyebrow raised.

"Lucky. Allow me to introduce you to John McCarthy, the owner of this fine establishment. John, this is Lucky Phillips, the young photographer I told you about last night at dinner."

John shook my hand and waved me to the other chair that he pulled up to the big wooden desk. "Yes, I've heard all about you."

"All good, I hope." Nervous, I could only think in clichés.

He smiled engagingly. "Surprisingly so. From all different directions."

The heat crept up on me and I sat down fast, almost missing the seat, but definitely dropping the prints. James scooted round and helped me pick them up with no fuss made. John watched me try to regain my footing. Once I sat back up, he asked, "Have you ever shown your work before? Published anything?"

"No, sir, I haven't. I've been working in a studio in Santa Fe for five years, and started learning more. But this is all new to me. A bit uncomfortable, aren't I?"

He nodded, with the smallest of smiles, and reached for the folder I'd laid on the table. He took out the first five prints. He spread them out across the tabletop and looked closely at each of them. The one of Michaela reaching for me. Christine on the swing. Chris studying at the table. The porch at Daniel's. The image of my boots waiting at the front door. His front door. He scrutinized each one, nodding to himself, occasionally looking up at James. He spoke to me though. "Do you have more like this?"

"Yes, I've taken almost two hundred in the last month. Since the end of October, I've been footloose; I left New Mexico, and found myself here. I've just documented the trip, that's all. The people I met on the way."

"And my neighbor, by the looks of it," John said with a grin.

James looked between us. "You know each other?"

"No, but remember I said someone came to the back door last night? It was Lucky here, asking for my sister. A new friend of hers, apparently. I didn't make the connection at the time."

I explained that I was staying next door with two students from the college. Chris and Joanna. How they'd taken me in for a few weeks until I decided whether to stay in Madison or go back to Santa Fe. And that I'd met Michaela when clearing snow from the driveways.

"And what have you decided?" asked John, curious to know more. "Are you staying?"

"I still haven't decided, to be honest. I'm not sure what to do. Do I need to stay to get ready for the show if you still want to do that?

When would that be? I have unfinished stuff to take care of in New Mexico, but nothing that can't wait." I kept it simple. I didn't tell them about my dad in hospital. I figured he'd be there for a long painfully slow time. I hadn't even told Chris or Michaela about him yet. I just couldn't make up my mind, that's what I told James and John. Later, I'd make up my mind later, I repeated to myself.

"Well, I think John will agree that a show would be perfect for all of us," James said. "You have a remarkable eye for the unusual and the sensual. It would be a shame to keep it out of the public eye. I'm curious to see more, some earlier work to see how you've come to this point. I'd also love to sit down and hear the stories behind each shot. See how lucky you really are!" James picked up the picture of Daniel. "For example, who is this old man? What made you want to capture him sitting on the porch of that beat-up house?"

I talked about how I'd met him at a pub in Custer, the bartender's jokes, and of the ease with which I'd chatted to them all; I ended up staying for a couple of days with Daniel at his place in town. I described the box of black and white photographs. How I'd stayed with him after that and chopped firewood for him. I told them how I helped out, talked for hours with Daniel each night, and hiked in the woods with his dogs in the mornings. "Just what I needed, being a country kid at heart."

"Did you grow up in the country?" James asked.

"No, not really. I had grandparents in Colorado, near Pagosa Springs, but I grew up all over the place. Dad was in the army most of my childhood so we ended up in England, and in Germany, as well as North Carolina and Albuquerque, of all places. The cities didn't agree with me. I left them as soon as I could."

"How is it being here? Madison is pretty big in comparison, isn't it?"

"Compared to Santa Fe, yes, but the Willy Street neighborhood feels like a village; we all say hello, help each other out, push cars stuck in the snow, that kind of thing. I see the neighbors at the co-op, at the coffee shop. I like running along the lakes, too. I'm loving being near water. But no, when I came up here, I didn't have a clear goal. A couple of weeks later and I'm still here with a bunch more photos to play with, and new friends to hang out with. It's pretty cool." I smiled nervously. There was a pause, kinda awkward when my words ran dry.

Luckily, James spoke up. "I'd say, back to your question about a show here at Stone Gallery, we'd aim for January. Probably the first week, a celebration of new talent and a new year. How does that sound?" James took out his calendar. "Yes, that should be ideal. We have another opening in December. We like to focus on one new artist per month. Would January work for you, Lucky?"

I grinned widely and nodded my head.

John agreed that the timing would be perfect. "I'd like to see the other images James has downloaded. But first things first. Can we go have lunch at the Italian restaurant up the road, do you think? And then come back and get down to the details? I'd like to hear more of your travels, Lucky, but I am truly hungry."

"What is the story behind this one?" James held out the photo from my home on Manhattan. The pile of Susan's belongings lay scattered on the roadside, lit only by the street lamp above, and the sign I'd scrawled was propped on the box nearest the drive.

I sighed. "Do you really need to know? I thought you wanted them to stand alone, James?" I said it lightly, but felt it deeply. There would be some photos best left alone.

He stared at me with a slight smile, and raised his glasses to look at me more clearly. "Is there something you'd rather not talk about?"

"Of course! Don't we all want to keep some things inside?"

John laughed. "Too late. We're curious now. The implied power of fights with lovers and strangers in these images is all part of their charm. The overall experience of leaving home, crossing the country alone and finding a new life—it's one we all dream of at times. You caught it on camera. You experienced what so many think about but never have the fire to act on. This is a story to be told. Even if we don't let others know the tale, we have a series of images to capture an archetypal journey. Loss. Grief. Anger. Love. All of it, right, Lucky?"

What could I say? The photos did tell the story of Susan walking away from me, the fight with Mike, him lying crumpled on the floor of the Cowgirl Bar in Santa Fe, me dumping Susan's belongings on the road in the middle of the night, the empty woods where I last saw Blue, prowling the warehouses late one night at the railyard, the main entrance to the hospital from when I last visited Dad, and then all of the empty highways across New Mexico. The truckers at Hooker, Oklahoma. The interstate through Kansas. The mess of road works in Missouri. The truck bashed in after that little side adventure in Iowa. So many snippets of my life since losing everything.

"And it seems to me you've found love again," teased John, holding the photo of Christine up to the light. "Or at least a lover."

She did look incredibly carefree and happy at the park. John held out the others of both Michaela and Chris, seeming to take it for granted it was the same woman. He didn't recognize the bedroom. The one in his own house. "Will she sign releases? Will any of your subjects have a problem with the show?"

I said I'd work it out later. I didn't know how, but I'd try. I asked how necessary it was to get releases. "Even the ones of candid shots—do I need releases for them, too? Like in the diner and all? Or the hand?"

"No, it's more the recognizable ones, faces, homes, anything like that can get you in trouble legally. It's worth taking the releases with you and get the signatures." John added that since the gallery was his, he was concerned that everything stays above board. His reputation was at stake, as a reliable source of new talent.

"What about the ones from Santa Fe, do I need to get them to sign them, too? They won't know any better."

"You'll need to contact them. I take it that you stay in touch with all these people? They are quite revealing images, Lucky. It pays to get permission."

Jen came in with a pot of coffee and set us up. John and James started to go through the images again, talking to each other of the merits and challenges of each one.

18

Susan and I had fought over those photos. Although the first night we got together, I'd told her how I love to take candid shots, and that I hoped she was okay with that. Susan had just laughed and touched me on the arm softly. "Yeah, we can do that. Promise me not to show anyone else, okay?"

I'd smiled and pulled out the camera and showed her, she took it from me and took one of me, grinning inanely in the throes of my new crush. She caught it exactly, the stupid smile on my face, a beer in hand, and the campfire behind us. *Click.*

We'd met at my friend's land up on the mesa, forty acres of thick forest, huge open meadows and a horizon that dwarfed the humans within it. She wore tight black jeans, a yellow t-shirt with the bar's logo, and her hiking boots. A cowboy hat framed her face. A half moon hung overhead and I'd pointed out the Milky Way to her, holding her hand in mine. The party carried on around us but I'd felt the world drift away. I'd held her hand in mine as we'd explored the barn, the fields, the paths, the stony hills, and sandy arroyo up in the hills.

Click. I'd taken two shots of her, sleeping naked in the outdoors, free and relaxed, totally trusting in the safety of both the mesa and me. She'd woken at the sound, but had smiled sleepily and drifted off almost immediately again. It was one of my favorite images of her. So stunningly innocent. In the morning, we'd returned to the campfire, for coffee and teasing from her friends.

Months later, I'd come home to find her in my house, with the laptop in front of her. She looked up at me. Her eyes streamed and her face was blotchy from crying.

"What? What's happened?" I came to her but she pushed my hand off, pointing to the screen in front. There I saw other photos. Images I'd taken of other lovers. Naked backs, thighs, hands and feet entwined.

"What? Those are private, Susan. What are you doing? I promised I'd never show them to anyone." I was furious. So was she.

"Like the ones of me? Of us making love? At White Sands? Or at the mesa? Did you show them to anyone or is it just for your own pornographic needs? You're a pervert, Lucky. What's with you? Why do you do this? Do they know you have these?"

"Yes, why wouldn't they? I never lied to anyone about them. Why are you so mad?"

"You just don't get it, do you?"

"No, obviously I don't. What's the fucking big deal here? I take photos. You know it. You said it was okay."

"I didn't know you'd add me to your collection. Is that all I am? Another body to steal?"

"Steal? You're joking, right?"

"No. I'm not. You stole those pictures of me. I was sleeping! I feel…I feel like you—"

"What? Like I what?"

Susan stood up. "Delete them all."

"All?"

"Yes, your other girlfriends, too. All of them."

I couldn't believe it. I pulled out the camera. I held it out to her.

There's nothing to it, I told her. You can delete all you like. She took it from me and turned it on. I watched her go through one by one, looking at them, the women I'd loved in one way or another, and then she deleted the whole memory. She turned back to the laptop. "Those, too."

I shrugged. "Whatever."

I walked out, taking my camera with me. *Click.* I shut the door.

She'd never found the memory stick in the drawer next to my bed.

19

I walked down State Street and found myself at the bar overlooking the lake. It was a surprisingly warm and sunny afternoon. I'd been in that office for some four hours.

We'd worked out most of the details. John had chosen ten images and James another fifteen. All in all, they'd decided on a series starting from the photo of Susan's note to me on the mirror. Up to and including my time on Willy Street with Chris and Michaela. I hadn't given any names. I simply promised to bring back releases within the month. Thanksgiving was coming up fast, and they had another show to focus on. I had time. How I'd do it, I still hadn't worked out, but I knew this was a chance in a lifetime.

I sat at the table nearest the marina and smoked. I drank back the Jim Beam, hard and fast. I no longer choked each time. Perhaps it was the practice. A daily practice. I smoked and stared out absent-mindedly.

"Can I join you?" Michaela stood across the table from me, wrapped in her suede jacket and a dark green fleece hat pulled down, her hair tied back, for once. She smiled and offered me another glass full of whiskey. "I saw you from inside so I thought we could have a drink together. I don't have any more classes today. What are you up to?"

"Is that it? I haven't seen you for a week, no messages worth mentioning, and you join me for a drink?"

"Yes. That's it exactly." She raised her glass to me and I couldn't help but laugh at her nerve. "So, how are you, Lucky? What's going on in your life? Apart from playing with my neighbor, that is! Are you having fun in town?"

"Yeah, I am, surprisingly. A great few days. I met your brother today. Nice man!"

"You did? Did you go over to the house again? Sorry, but I had an early morning class with the freshmen."

"No—at the gallery," I told her. I described Daniel's photo box, the need to capture images, and how I was going to have a show in the New Year. I told her a shorthand version of the story of that week in Custer, and she asked me for more details. This was what I was drawn to, her understanding of passion, and this focus for more than work and home and television. She thrived on talk of art. Of desire. Of needs undefined. She understood. She understood me. We talked for an hour or so before she shivered.

"I'm hungry," she stated and stood up. "Let's go out for dinner. Do you like Indian? There's a great place on the west side. I'll drive us."

In the car, she asked about Christine, curious and apparently not at all jealous. She turned on the radio to a station playing salsa and merengue. I liked it. I told her how Chris and I hang out and play. Nothing serious. And her? Did she have a new lover?

Yes, she did, the older guy I'd seen her with the other day out at the college. Donald. Another professor. I cringed. I couldn't help it. I didn't like to share. I fell silent.

She laughed at me and ignored the bad mood, chatting away about Thanksgiving, her family coming for the weekend. "What are you doing for the holidays, Lucky?"

We pulled in at the restaurant. I didn't answer. I held open the door for her and we walked in to a quiet family run place, a typical Westerner's idea of Indian styles and music. This would be the second meal out in one day. How I put it all away, I didn't know.

I led us to a booth at the back near the tall windows. Outside, the streets teemed with commuter traffic. *Click.* She undid her jacket and hung it on the peg nearby. I put the camera between us. Michaela picked it up. "May I?"

I nodded. I wanted to see her reaction to the images of her. I didn't know how to ask her permission to show them. She focused on the one of Mike on the floor at the pub. She stared at me with an eyebrow raised. I shook my head and ordered two beers.

"What happened to him?" she asked.

"Later. I'll explain later," I told her. She held the image out to me again but I shook my head and sipped my beer. I wanted to go out for a smoke. I didn't. I waited. She asked again.

"Mike, isn't it? Is that something you did to him, Lucky? It looks like quite the fight. What happened?"

The waiter came up just then, though, and we focused on our orders. Then he left us to it. I finished my beer. She didn't give me a break and asked once more, "Have you spoken to him since then?"

"No, I don't want to. He called the other day, though. Left me a message. Seems to think it's no big deal to go off with my girlfriend."

"Ah. Jealous type, are you?"

What could I say? Nothing. I asked about Donald.

She laughed out loud. "I don't think you really want to know, do you? How about we talk about the holiday? I'm excited to have my nieces and nephew coming with my parents. Yes, good old Mom and Dad are coming down from Minnesota to visit their kids. Admittedly, we make it easy for them, since John and I like living together. It should be quite the gathering. And you? What are you doing?"

"Nothing that I know of. I don't even know if I'll be here. I might go back to New Mexico after all."

"Really? Why?"

"In part, I need to get releases for some of the photos, but mostly, I never planned on settling again, let alone living with anyone again. I think it's time to leave."

"Even if you like Christine?"

"Well, that's what usually happens. By chance. I like someone. I fall into something with her. But, well, right now, I kinda need to be alone. Single."

Michaela snorted into her beer. "Right, Lucky. Like you didn't come home with me. That's not being alone. Or single! Spending all these days with me, in my bed, in my kitchen. That's not being alone. You know that, don't you?"

"Yeah, but you know what I mean. We're just playing with sex, that's all, right? And Chris and I are playing house. It's a whole different game. Not one that I want."

"Because of Susan and Mike?" I

shook my head.

Luckily, the food came right then and her focus shifted. We both tucked in, talking about our past lovers and the ups and downs of relationships. She teased me about being too intense and attached. So what if Mike and Susan got together? Hadn't I been friends with him since we'd been teenagers? Well, true, I said, but…

She cut me off. Friends piss each other off, she told me, and then they get over it. Not a big deal in the long run.

"But he betrayed me!" I said. "My trust. How can I trust him again? I told him everything, and look what he did. I can't let it go. It's too messed up. I can't trust him. He's a selfish fucker. Simple as that."

"And you've never lied, yourself? Cheated? None of that?"

"No, I haven't."

She raised her beer bottle to me. "So, Christine knows we've had sex? And how often? And how great it is? Or what you do for me? When she's next door, and when you've come over—she knew about all that?"

I sipped my beer. "Well, not exactly. But that's different!"

"How? Do tell, Lucky! Because I think, if she knew, she'd say you're being dishonest. And what's the difference between lying, dishonesty, and holding back? Isn't it the same thing?"

I couldn't answer that. She was right. If Michaela invited me back to her home in the next five minutes, I'd be hard pushed to say no. I shrugged. "What do you think of the photos?"

She let me redirect us. She picked up the camera again and turned it on. "They're vague, like you can't tell really what was going on, and I like that quality. The angles and the sensual aspect. I can see why John liked them. And who's this?"

"Susan."

"Ahh.' Michaela looked more closely at the small screen. "Is that her walking away from you?"

"Yep. Thanks for pointing that out."

She smiled slyly and scrolled ahead, past the road trip shots of empty gas stations, motel rooms full of my belongings unpacked. She focused on the women. The bodies coming and going into focus. She turned off the camera and handed it back to me. "Yes, you'll make quite an impression. Very graphic, in a PG kind of way."

"Is that a complement?"

"Yes, it is. Revealing of how you are with your lovers, and of your anger toward them, too. Yet, you're careful, not too explicit. I like them. I'm curious to see which photos get shown. What John and James chose. I'll wait and see. Don't tell me, okay? Now, what about the holidays? Are you going to stay with Christine? Or are you going home? See your family?"

I stood up, left forty bucks on the table, and put on my coat. "Time for a smoke?"

She joined me outside and we stood under the porch, watching the traffic and not talking. The lights came on around us, and the night chill attacked us. I pulled out the camera and took a shot of us both together. Posed for once.

Michaela turned to me. "Let's go home. Stay with me for the night, Lucky. We never have woken up with each other. I'd like that. And then you can tell me the rest."

20

"What are you doing next week?"

I don't know, I told her, as I brought in an armful of firewood. I stacked it by the rest. I cleaned up the kindling pile. I brushed off my fleece and took my work boots off, laying them neatly by the fire to dry off. I stretched out and picked a few soggy leaves from my jeans. Christine watched me carefully. And then she asked me, "Why won't you talk much? You never mention your family, do you, Lucky?"

I sat back on my haunches and sighed. "I don't know. I just don't like to, that's all."

"My parents are coming to stay. Mom wants to meet you."

Oh, crap. Both sets of parents at the same time? Next door? I couldn't breathe.

"Want a drink?" I walked into the kitchen and grabbed the Jim Beam and poured myself a shot. I drank another.

"Isn't it a bit early to drink?" Her voice came from the doorway as she watched me.

"Really? I thought I was a grown up here, got to do what I like."

She stared at me, and then walked out of the kitchen and into her bedroom, softly closing the door behind her. She hadn't asked me about last night. I hadn't offered. The tension had grown all afternoon as she'd followed me with her eyes. I'd cleaned up the kitchen, tidying up as I do. The piles of dirty cups drove me nuts. I washed out the fridge, too, wiping it down, and taking out the trash. I went and had a shower. No message for me on the mirror. Not yet, anyway.

I'd glanced out the window, wondering what Michaela was up to. You see, I'd come back over here once I saw Chris and Joanna leave for school in the morning. I'd come back over and made the fire, took out my laptop and worked on the photos. Working on the titles. On an order for the show. Naming and numbering. I started recreating my artist statement, editing it again and again. James had appreciated the first version but he wanted 150 words not the thirty I'd offered. I filled out some details, the trip, coming from New Mexico, the experience of showing the story and not holding it inside. I fit it all into one page as requested.

By the time I'd finished, both Chris and Joanna had come back from town. Arms full of grocery bags and not a word was said. Joanna looked from me to Christine and then silently disappeared into her room. I'd cleaned up my notes, put away the food and sat back down in front of the fire. After a half hour or so, Chris came and sat in the armchair opposite me, with a mug of hot chocolate. Neither of us spoke.

But then I looked at her. She wiped her eyes, and sipped her drink, staring into the flames. I poked them. Not her.

"Are you hungry?" I asked. "I could make you something."

She shook her head but still said nothing. I wanted a shot of Jim, but I didn't do it. She'd made it clear what she thought about that idea. I leaned forward with my hands on my knees and stared into the fire with her.

And I started to tell her a story. My story. "My Mom died when I was a kid, she was in a car crash and died right there. I was at school. They didn't tell me until the end of the day. The teacher held me back after class. She sat me down. I was ten. She sat me down in the seat in the back by the window. I remember thinking I was in trouble again. I wasn't a great kid at school. Mischievous, you know?" I looked up and saw Chris watching me intently. "Mrs. Thomas told me Mom had been in an accident on the motorway to London. Brake failure in the commuter traffic. We were living at the army base outside of Witney, near Oxford. It was raining. I noticed the dripping trees, and the leaves on the playground, huge piles of soggy dead autumn leaves. I focused on the sound of the water. Mrs. Thomas told me that Dad was coming to pick me, but wouldn't be here for another half an hour. She'd offered to wait with me in the classroom. I didn't get it. I asked if I could go outside to play. No, sorry Lucky, but you have to stay with me, she said trying to—I don't know what. Maybe she was scared I'd run away again? I don't know.

"We waited. She kept trying to get me to talk. But I had nothing to say. I sat there and watched the rain. Dad came in, drenched, pale, his hair slicked back with the rain. He held out his hand for me and I stood up and walked over. He said something to Mrs. Thomas but I didn't hear him. He held my hand and we walked out."

I stood up and went to get a drink. It was early afternoon. Cocktail hour somewhere in the world, right? I came back, though, and sat down. Chris said nothing. She sipped her drink, not really watching me, just there, curled up in beat-up and faded gray sweats. Quiet. I liked that. I relaxed back into the sofa. She joined me, the cushions giving way to her weight. Chris held my hand and stroked my face. Wasn't this how it all started? With her and me? Tenderness is my undoing.

I closed my eyes. She leaned next to me and curled up around me. Still silent. Joanna crept past us and out the front door. I listened to the wood burn. I smelled shampoo and soap. I smelled the Jim Beam on my breath. Chris stroked my hair, my face, and my mouth. And yes, we kissed. Not the passion of the other lover I knew so well. But there was a deep knowing, acceptance of each other at that very moment.

I craved the camera but knew not to. I opened my eyes. So did she. We sat back. The next few hours passed quietly. I said little, just to ask after food or drinks or heat. Christine said nothing to me. Nodded occasionally but that was it.

"Have you thought about whether you're staying for Thanksgiving?" she asked me, finally.

"Not really. It's too cold to drive the truck back like it is so I'm not sure what I'll do. I'll work it out later."

"You can stay here, until after Thanksgiving. But that's it. After that, you have to decide what you want. Who you want."

I stilled instantly.

"Yes, I know about you and Professor McCarthy. I saw you." I turned to her quickly.

"No, don't try to deny it. I know, Lucky. I know." She messed with her hair nervously and put down the empty mug. "More whiskey?"

I nodded. She left. I waited for another five minutes before she brought me the bottle. She had another cup of tea. She sat down in the armchair, distant from me.

"Why today? Why today that you finally talk to me? Tell me more than the charming stories mixed with some heartbreak? I don't get it. You spent the night next door. Next door. With my teacher. Then you come back to me and open up. What the hell goes on in your mind, Lucky? Why now? When my parents are coming? When the holidays are coming? Oh, Christ. I can't believe it." Harsh words spoken in such a soft voice that I almost missed them. I leaned forward, trying to hear her. I didn't know what to say. I didn't need to.

"How long, Lucky?" she went on. "Have you been with her all this time? And you didn't tell me? When I asked you if you liked her, you shrugged it off, made a joke of it. But? Well? Have you been with her this whole time? I feel like such a fool. How am I supposed to go to class with her on Friday? Does she know about us? Oh, Christ. Fuck."

She sat back and stared at the ceiling. I wanted to ask about how or rather when she saw me with Michaela. Could I ask? Would it be rude beyond belief? I wanted to smoke. I knew though that if Michaela saw me outside she'd come out to join me. Not what I needed right now. What to say? What to say?

"I'm sorry."

Chris laughed at me harshly. "For what? Getting caught lying to me? For being busted? For telling me about your mom when it's not what's on my mind or yours? I don't get it. When I said you were holding back, I didn't realize how much." She sat back and closed her eyes. "Is there more I need to know?"

I didn't dare move. But I couldn't help it. I reached for the camera.

"Don't you dare."

I stopped.

"Talk to me, Lucky. If you want to save this, whatever this is to you, you have to talk."

"I wasn't lying to you, Christine."

"Oh? So what do you think it is when you don't tell the whole truth? That's not honesty in my book."

"But I didn't lie, I'm not dishonest. I'm not."

She laughed again, but softly this time, to herself. "Give me that Jim Beam." I passed it over and she poured a huge shot into her tea. "Detox tea. Funny, huh?"

I poured another shot for myself. I tried to explain that holding things back, it's different. It's not breaking trust. It's not being dishonest. She wouldn't, couldn't hear it. Found it laughable that I thought that way. She was insulted to think I hadn't told her everything.

I turned on her. "And you? Have you told me everything? Or told your friends everything? I doubt it. We all hold in stories. Tell some. Hold others. Right?" My anger was bubbling up. Jim Beam was stirring in me. I sat upright. "Have you ever liked two people at the same time? For very different reasons?"

"Yes."

"And?"

"I didn't act on it. I didn't fuck them both."

Apparently, Jim was stirring us both up. A part of me woke up after a long slumber. The rage at Susan kicked my shins, demanding for me to yell, scream, and get it out. Either that or implode.

Chris suddenly looked at me, hard and long. "What? What, Lucky? You want to fight me like you did with Susan? Or with Mike? Is that what gets you going? That and taking photos? I just don't get you."

Jim Beam ran away and I deflated. Slightly. I sat back and tensed my shoulders, arms, fists, but then shook myself out. I poked the fire again.

"It's fine. Will you stop doing that?"

I stopped. Not sure what to do with myself. Not sure what to say, if anything. "Chris. I'm sorry." I paused. "I like you. I like Michaela. It's different with each of you. Honest. It's nothing personal."

Yes, she laughed bitterly and reached for the bottle again. I went outside for a cigarette. Still light out. I'd expected night to have fallen. Aren't most fights at night? The lights were on next door but I hoped for once not to see Michaela. We'd had an amazing night together, one of the best nights so far; great loving, funny conversations and we'd slept entwined with each other. Perfect. And now I wanted more of her. Michaela, though, was quite happy with what we had. Not attached, as she pointed out to me. Not a big deal to her. How come? I'd asked her, but she'd just shrugged and drew me back into the sheets with her. The curtains had been open. Was that it? Her bedroom faces Christine's house, maybe even her room. I hadn't thought of that before. I hadn't looked. Oh, hell. What do I do? I thought. Do I even have a choice?

Back inside, Chris was in the kitchen, heating up some leftovers from a few nights ago. Chicken soup. Good for the mood? I went back inside, I got out two bowls. She served us both and we sat at the table. One on each side.

I ate a spoonful. "Do you want me to leave?"

"Is that what you expect? Is that what you usually do?"

"No, it's my girlfriends, they leave me. Not the other way around." But I was lying. Susan was the first to leave me.

"Really? Why? You only told me about Susan cheating on you with your friend, Mike, right?" Chris actually looked at me with some level of curiosity instead of hatred.

I risked it. "Yeah, well, they leave me for various reasons. Not for cheating, though. Honest. More like they tell me that they don't know me after all. No idea what makes me tick. Kinda what Susan said, too, she said I was too hard to get close to. Didn't give her enough. I don't know." I drank a glass of water.

"Well, I don't run away." She ate more soup and filled my bowl again. I didn't want it, but couldn't say no in case it pissed her off. I said a nice, polite thank you.

"Sure," she answered. "But I mean it: You have until after Thanksgiving. You have to decide what you want, or rather *who* you want, by that weekend. If it's not here, trying to make this work, then you need to find yourself another place, another home and girlfriend."

"So I can stay?"

"Yes, on the couch. I'm not having you in my bed unless you really want to be there." She pointed her fork at me. "I'm not a prude about sharing lovers, but if I'm going to break my promise to myself about taking this year to focus solely on studying, and instead I end up getting together with you, it's got to be real. Deep. No playing games with me, Lucky."

I nodded and drank more water. I didn't ask for more than that. She took the bowls and threw them into the sink with the pans and spoons.

"When my parents are here, you'll have to share the front room with me. They'll be in my room. I'll take the couch. You sleep on the floor. No funny stuff. Okay?"

She left the room. I stood up. I did the dishes. I wiped down the counters. I wanted to smoke but I didn't dare go outside so I just went to bed.

21

"You don't love me and I know it now. No. I know it," Susan had said to me over the running bath water. I'd held my head over the sink. I stood there in my striped shorts and black t-shirt with another hangover. Too often those days. Susan raised her voice. "What were you two thinking? Going out to Albuquerque and driving back like that? Get a fucking motel next time you're so lit that you can't see straight. Get a hooker, I don't care. Just don't come back here."

"It's my home."

"Thanks for reminding me, Lucky! And what about Mike? What did he do to you to get you so pissed at him? I don't get you two. You've known each other for what?—fifteen years or so? And the way you two fight and bicker, it's like you're both still kids!"

"I don't remember. Were we fighting when we got home? Huh. No idea. I'll ask him when he wakes up."

"Great. Another morning with the both of you dirty and drunk. You'd better not be late to work again. You'll lose your job at the studio. He's warned you."

"What's this about, Susan? My not loving you?" The bathroom lights struck me hard, and I opened the curtains. It was completely calm and quiet outside, no neighbors talking, no cars driving by. The view was of the apricot trees in full leaf, the remains of the year's fruit fallen on the dirt below. Blue lay in the shady spot in the far corner. I focused back on my girlfriend. She stood a few inches smaller than me, pretty in a librarian kind of away, geeky, you know? She was dressed once again in the tidy, and almost formal black suit-pants and white shirt, unbuttoned to show a hint of cleavage. Her blond hair looked different.

"Did you cut your hair?"

"Yes. And you know why?" I

shook my head.

"We had a date last night. Or I did. I waited at Il Vicino for an hour, had two glasses of cabernet before I gave up. I even tried calling you. No answer. I came over to the Cowgirl to see if you were there. The bartender told me you'd both gone to see a band in Albuquerque. That was great, Lucky. Thanks."

"But it's not our anniversary. Is it?"

"No. Of course not. That was June. Don't you remember? You brought me a whole bunch of red roses you'd cut in the middle of the night from the park by Mike's house. I thought it was so romantic of you! What a joke!"

"No, honey, Susan. I'm sorry we got drunk. I forgot. But—"

"Yeah?"

I do love you, I told her, turning off the taps so I could hear myself think. I love you, I told her again and again, pulling her against me. "My beautiful friend. I do love you." I murmured it over and over again, making her giggle as my breath tickled her neck, my hands wandering all over. "You'd better tell your boss you'll be late."

"Oh yeah? And why?" And with that I gently pushed us both into the bath, fully clothed and squealing in shock.

22

At a coffee shop on State Street, I opened my computer along with everyone else. I remember the days when we all sat and chatted to each other. That's all changed. Lost in our own worlds.

I plugged in, checked my email. Music played in the distance. Muzac as far as I was concerned. It all sounded the same. I didn't recognize anything—been too long without a radio. That truck of mine, you know? Not the best place for listening to music. Well, there's an am radio. That's it, though. Great for evangelical diatribes against people like me. Blah blah, I can't stand them.

Constant music in the background? When we lived together, I'd been surprised to find that Susan had been over too: Her job at the radio station had taken away all of her interest in more music. Funny. She'd liked the peace and quiet of us alone at home. Even a night out to see a band no longer appealed to her. I used to go with Mike. I missed that. I missed Mike. The fucker.

Online, I found out it would cost me about $235 for a train back and forth to Lamy, just outside Santa Fe. Could I get a ride from there? Or should I risk it with the truck? Would Hilda make it? I'd figure it out later. I wanted to go back. Talking about Mom the other night had stirred it all up. I wanted to talk to my Dad. See if he could hear me, know me, I didn't know. I hadn't kept in touch with the doctors. The ICU. The ward. Hospice. Whatever you call it. They couldn't do anything without me. So I knew where to find him, hooked up to those machines.

A long time ago, Dad had told me about a sister. A sister of mine, that is. In Arizona. I'd never met her. Maybe I could find her? How, though, was a different matter. Now that I'd decided to go back, it all came to me. Family. Thanksgiving. What did I have left? My mom had been dead for decades. My Dad was unable to move, talk, or do anything for himself. And I had a sister I didn't know, had never even thought about. The best dog in the world was lost in the mountains. And my friends? Who knew? I almost emailed Mike. But I didn't. I wrote to Michaela, instead.

We met a couple of hours later. She picked me up at the coffee shop and we drove out of town. We headed north. Nothing to it, really, I'd just asked if she wanted to go to a lake or a river or something. Yes, give me an hour, she'd said. I waited a bit longer than that but I didn't care. I hadn't seen her for a few days. Or nights.

She grabbed me from behind and bit my ear quickly before I had a chance to turn around.

"Let's go! I had class but now I'm done for a whole week and I want to celebrate! My parents come tomorrow, so this is perfect, Lucky. Let's go." She held out my leather to me and packed up the laptop, taking it with her. I put the mug in the bussing tray on the way out, saying bye to the barista.

I had to run to catch up with Michaela. She strode ahead, telling me about this river campsite she hadn't been to for ages. It'll be frozen on the edges by now, she told me as we climbed into her car. "I can't wait. I need to get out of town for a moment. Take a breath of fresh air. Smoke?" She handed me her pack, asking me to light one for her, too. I smiled to myself and lit one for each of us. I hadn't had a cigarette since that fight with Christine. I hadn't drunk anything, either. Oh, well. Old dogs and all of that.

We listened to Anthony and the Johnsons and smoked, driving up the highway, with her pointing out different places she knew, or had been to. Then we were in the woods, with no or very little traffic. Trees blocked the views so I watched Michaela's profile. She didn't ask me any personal questions, just about the show and working with her brother.

"He's been great," I told her. "Very helpful, telling me the best way to word things. I get tongue-tied around him, but I like him. He's smart, very quick."

"He likes you, too."

"Really?" I grinned. I liked hearing that.

"I do, too, in case you didn't know."

I touched her face gently. "Want to show me how much?"

"No, not like that! I mean it, Lucky. I like talking to you." I took my hand away.

"Oh my God, you're an insecure one, aren't you? Put your hand back!"

I did.

"I like talking to you because you have great stories. I know you're holding back on me, but I like that. The enigma of you. The mystery. And the rage I sense. You've hurt people in the past, haven't you?"

"What do you mean?" I took my hand away and focused on flicking ash out the window.

"I like the danger. I like fucked up relationships." She laughed out loud. Manic today, Michaela scared me a little. I didn't know what to say. She carried on anyway. "And I have a feeling you like that, too. Fighting and making up. We haven't had a fight yet, have we?"

I shook my head, hoping she wasn't about to start something in the car. We pulled off the highway onto a side dirt track, heading into a mass of trees and leaves. No one had been down there for a long time by the state of the tracks. I glanced all around us.

"Don't worry," she said, "this little car can take us to the river. It's only a mile and we can park. Do you have more matches?"

"For a campfire?"

Michaela nodded as she downshifted, coming around a tight corner. The woods made the afternoon draw to a close and I wished I'd worn more layers. We stopped next to a huge oak tree, half burned by lightning. The path led us past a stand of shrubs, barren of leaves or flowers. We held hands and Michaela took me with her. I followed, listening for the river. We came to the ice-covered beach. A pile of rocks made a campfire and she turned to me, smiling widely. "I used to come here all the time when I was a student. I loved this place. I mean, on the weekends it was a party place, full of frat boys and the like. But during the week, in the mornings, it was so quiet I'd see deer, rabbits, and so many incredible birds. It was my refuge. I wanted you to see it. I came to read, to study, and I'd make a fire and do just that. A flask of rum or tea. Welcome to my other world, Lucky."

She stuck her arms out like a proud little kid at show and tell, and took me around the clearing to the water's edge.

We set about making a huge fire to warm us. The early night was growing dark. I found armfuls of dead and down wood. She pulled over two tree trunks for us to sit on. We sat next to each other, my arms around her as she talked of her school days, the times alone and the times with the other students. A mix of solitary and social, Michaela had mostly fit into college life, but missed the expanse of Minnesota, so came here to be alone.

"Not with lovers?" I teased.

She shook her head. "Generally me, myself and I. Or so the song goes, right? You remember that one, don't you?"

"Joan Armatrading?"

"Yes, I always loved her stuff. Especially in the mid-'80s. Do you like music?"

"I don't really think about it, to be honest. I hear it. I don't listen, though. It's just there, you know?"

We chatted about the kinds of music we remembered from being teenagers, from our twenties. The strangely popular New Wave movement and big hairdos. The grunge bands and scruffy clothes from the northwest. We even talked briefly about politics, but we agreed too much, so there wasn't much to talk about. We carried the same basically liberal and socialist ideals. I told about my experiences in the Deep South, how I'd felt outnumbered by the Baptists and how scared that had made me. I didn't mention my more recent encounters on the way through the Midwest. I explained how I couldn't cope with the duality of the southern hospitality and the fear I'd carried with me all those years ago, so I hadn't stuck around.

"When were you there?"

"Sometime in the '90s, I was in my mid-twenties, a scruffy hippy kid with a backpack, looking for odds and ends of jobs. Nah, not great. I lasted a month at most and then hitchhiked north. Much more my style. Chicago. That was a fun city."

"I was there at the Art Institute for a few months. But I didn't like the city. I baled out. I left. My dad never understood that. He's proud of me now, I think. Being a teacher suits his hopes for me. And John having the gallery, well, let's say my parents are quite pleased with their offspring."

"Doesn't John have kids? Do you?"

"No, I don't. He was married and got divorced; let's see, about three years ago. They're still good friends, he and Deb, but not together. They have three kids, two girls and a boy. They're coming to spend Thanksgiving with us. Teenagers by now." She turned to me and asked again, "What are you doing for Thanksgiving? What about your own family? Are you and Christine still together?"

"No, not really. I'm back on the sofa." I gave a quick shrug.

She sat back, "What happened? Are you okay? I know I gave you a hard time the other day, but—"

I poked the fire. "She saw us together. I don't know when. But she told me she saw us."

"That explains her absence today, then." Michaela took the stick out of my hand. "And you? How are you doing with that? With all of this?"

"Fine. Just fine." I pulled out my tobacco and a flask of Jim. "Want some?"

We turned back to the flames, and watched as the early low half moon came up over the trees. She talked about art. An easy subject for us both. We laughed over her experiments at the Art School. She described the sculptures made of recycled objects, but all she had lying around her apartment were empty beer cans. She failed that class. She was even sent to a counselor for her tendency toward drug abuse. At that point, though, she told me she'd realized that Chicago, or rather that school, wasn't the place for her.

She turned to me and held my face in her hands. She stared at me in the firelight. Turning me this way and that. Scrutinizing me. Finally, she gave me a gentle kiss. Her tongue probed into my mouth, exploring me, but for once without the bite I'd grown used to. Softer. Michaela was gentle with me. Unnerving. Most unsettling.

I responded, anyway.

"Do you have kids, Lucky?"

"No, I wanted to, but it never happened. Never found the right place or person. I like them, just not in my daily life, I guess. You? Did you ever want any?"

She smiled. "No, too selfish. I like my life as it is. I like having my lovers." Plural. That made me shift on my tree trunk. "And I like my friends over for dinner," she went on. "I'm pretty happy with what I have going on. And you, Lucky?"

I shook my head. "Not yet. I'm working on it. But right now? No."

She kissed me again. Passionately. Aggressively. "Well, let's get you out of your head, shall we?"

23

I walked up to the lake park and sat on the swings. I pulled the leather closer around me, and put on my ever-present hat. I hadn't used the camera all week. I didn't know what had happened. Something had shifted and I didn't like it. John and James both stressed that I needed permission to take photos. But that spoiled it. Spontaneity turned me on. The hidden. The candid conversation of subject and camera. Now what was I going to do? Could I carry on, regardless?

The clouds crept over Lake Mendota slowly. I didn't pull out the tobacco. I kept it close, just in case. I hadn't had any Jim Beam for three days now. I'd had a couple of beers each afternoon, out at the terrace, but that was it. Trying to hold myself in check.

I'd been spending my evenings in front of the fire at Christine's, reading and writing. Nothing much. Quiet. Drained. The three of us, Chris, Joanna and I, ate dinners together. Mostly I cooked. Mostly I cleaned. They studied. I took care of things.

Conversations followed a superficial—to me—tone; they talked about school, the student union, and stories from the Isthmus, nothing of any deep nature. I didn't know what Joanna knew, but we all kept things light. The days passed. The parents were to arrive the next morning. Wednesday. Christine's parents. Michaela's were already next-door. I'd heard them in the kitchen the other afternoon.

I hadn't seen Michaela since the trip. We'd had one of those great nights together. But. I drank too much again. I'd come back to Christine's and had fallen asleep on top of my sleeping bag. Embarrassed to find that Chris had thrown a blanket over me during the night.

That morning, I cleaned the kitchen. I cleaned myself. I cleaned the inside of the Nissan, taking out trash, even washing the windshield. My poor truck. It was about time to put her out to pasture. Not yet. Later. Like I said, I washed her, shone her up, filled the tires, and changed her oil. I gave her a full tune up. Just in case it'd help. You never know, right?

I pulled out the camera. I scrolled back and forth. Uninspired. I kept thinking of Dad. I hadn't told Chris of my decision. Nor Michaela. I didn't know how. I didn't have the words. Perhaps I could show them? An image. To tell the story. The need in me to find Dad. My sister. An image. Yes, I needed to go out with camera in hand and find the story. Capture it. Show it.

I stood up and walked into town.

24

On the main streets around the Capitol building, I saw all kinds of people, some talking and some quiet, a mix of kids and adults alike out and about before the next storm kicked us down, some people jogging past me, others slowly making their way home clutching walking sticks, and a few kids were chasing each other across the lawns.

I sat on a bench and took shots of the families, of the smiles on one dad's face as he watched his boys running up to him with leaves in their hands. The mom with the stroller and a pile of bags on the kid's knees—she looked drained and sad. An old couple walked past me, both wrapped up to the ninth degree with hardly an inch of wrinkles showing. I caught them slowly crossing onto State Street, holding up the bus. I took one of a three- year-old, holding hands with two women, grinning up at them both. I took one of the teenage girl at the bus stop next to me, texting her friends as she listened to her Ipod. The bus came and she didn't break stride, her thumbs typing away as she climbed in. A white-haired man, wizened, frail, and wrapped tightly in layers against the freezing weather slowly stepped down from the bus. He had two walking sticks. He struggled with the last step, almost fell onto me and I threw out my hands toward him, catching his arms in mine. He held on tightly and leaned on me. The bus left us and the snow began.

"Do you need help getting somewhere?" I asked as he found his balance.

"Why, I'd like that, if you can. What's your name?" He peered up at me, and being barely able to focus on me, he pulled me in closer. "Let me see you, dammit."

I bent down to his shrunken height and let him hold my face, much as Michaela had done only days ago. The old man moved his fingers around the lines of my eyebrows, my smile and across my cheeks. "Healthy, are you? I can't tell. It seems like it. But you never can tell, can you?" He took his hands away from me and stood back a moment. "Where's your family from?"

"All over," I said, and asked again if he'd like me to walk with him.

"It's important to know these things. I know young people like you aren't interested, but our families tell us a lot. Especially at times like this."

"The snow you mean?" I asked.

He grunted. "No, Thanksgiving. The holidays. Where did you say you were from? Your accent isn't a local one. I'd know. I'm local born and bred. Some eighty-four years now. Can you believe it? Still going strong." He grunted again. He walked off to the west of the square, taking my arm in his, leaning on me. "I'm going to the building over there," he said, pointing to the apartments opposite the back of Stone Gallery. I nodded. I walked slowly.

"My name is Lucky. Glad to meet you."

"Well, you might not say much, but you're polite. Unlike so many these days!" he introduced himself as Frank Walker.

"Lucky Phillips."

We crossed at the lights. "Do you have family here, Lucky Phillips?"

"No," I shook my head. "I don't really have any family left."

Frank stopped walking and stared at me sadly. "I know the feeling. I know the feeling." His head shook slightly as he faced up at the snowflakes, sticking his tongue out. "There is still joy in the world, though, isn't there?"

"I'm not sure." I couldn't help but be honest with him.

We walked again, slowly creeping along the slippery sidewalk. Snow dripped into my collar and I shivered.

"Family. If no family, then you have good friends, I hope? Ones you've known all your life? Although, they'll be the next to go. It's not good to be so old and alone. You're young to be without family. I don't want to ask. But I hope that you have friends, Lucky. And something to live for. You have a long way to go, God willing."

I told him about Dad in hospital. About new friends here. He shook his head sadly. I told him about the camera, the photographs. I asked if I could take his portrait.

"Yes. Of course. I'd like that. How about here?"

Frank Walker stood by himself, unsteadily, under a lamppost, holding his two sticks, and with his hat pulled down low across his forehead. *Click.* The snow lay on his shoulders, on his hat, and even on his hands.

"What will you do with the photos?"

"I'll bring you copies, if you like. Would you?" Touched by his innocence and grumbly good offer of friendship, I wanted to do more. I didn't know what.

"Come in for tea. You can show me what you're doing. You can tell me about your dad. I'd like that."

"Black tea for you then, my friend?" He pottered around his kitchen, filling the kettle and setting it on the gas range. He lit it carefully. He sat down opposite me at the small metal table.

"Thanks for helping me off the bus. Some of those drivers get up and give me a hand; others, like today, close the door on me as soon as my foot leaves that last step. A couple of times I've lost a scarf to those impatient ones!" He smiled. "Let me get my glasses out and see your photos. May I, Lucky?"

"Yes, Frank, here you go. You press that little button to the left to scroll to the previous ones. Can you see it?"

He took the camera from me and fiddled for a few moments before looking up at me with a wide surprised look of delight.

"These are wonderful, my friend. Most wonderful!"

I turned red at his praise and that made him chortle to himself as he focused back on the images coming up. The kettle began to boil. I stood and took care of things. I poured the water on the PG Tips teabags, most proudly he'd pointed out that he drank nothing but the best English teas. A reminder of his army days in the U.K. In the early '70s, he'd lived there.

He took the mug I handed him, and carried on talking about the army base at Southampton. He'd stayed there for a month. He remembered it so clearly. Talking about the Rose and Crown, on the High Street, his local where all the army boys hung out on furlough. The local girls came and flirted, then skipped home singing loudly in their broad southern accents. Florence was one such lass, she married his best friend one summer, only six months before he died from what's now called 'friendly fire.'

Will I have such a good memory? Will I still be alive when I'm his age? I couldn't watch him, half scared I'd be him one day, and also suddenly realizing that it might all go, life, I might die any day and not know what it's like to be crippled by arthritis, needing glasses, or even walking sticks. I might not experience any of it. Not if I carry on like I had been. Right? Got to cut back. Do something differently. I didn't know what. Or how. I drank the strong tea, with milk and one sugar, as he suggested.

Frank took off his cardigan, handed back the camera and stretched gently against his chair. He smiled so innocently again. I had to take another photo. He knew. He saw me. He smiled more. And he drank his tea. He held out his hands to me.

"Take my hands in yours," he instructed me.

I put the camera down, and reached across the table to him. He held my hands. He stared me in the eyes. I looked around the cramped kitchen, blues and greens, framed photos, paintings, knick-knacks on every surface, the sink full of cleaned dishes. His home. I glanced back. He was still staring at me intently, but so gently. I looked out the window. Down at my tea. Back.

"What is it, Lucky? What are you afraid of?"

I began to cry; a tear dropped down my cheek and into the mug. Frank didn't let go of my hands. He held onto me. My face crumpled up. I couldn't look at him, at anything without my chin wobbling as I tried to talk, say something to change the focus. Sobbing, my head fell down and onto our hands, still held tight. Strong for an old man, he didn't complain. He didn't move. He stayed right there. He didn't let go.

"Talk to me, Lucky."

"I can't. I can't talk about it. It messes me up." I smiled weakly as Frank poured us another cup of tea.

"I think it's the *not* talking that is messing you up. Have you told anyone about your family? Talked about your dad with anyone?"

I shook my head slowly. I drank the piping hot tea and spat it out. Too hot. He laughed and passed me a dishtowel.

"Take your time, my friend. I have all the time in the world."

At that I looked at him, uncertain—was he joking? No, apparently not. Frank sat there like a Buddhist statue, all peace and warm hearts. I blew on the tea. I wanted to add Jim to the brew. I looked up at this strange old man and wondered how I'd ended up with him. Taking photos. Taking photos, that's what got me here. Damn cameras.

I sat up and started to talk. "Dad's had a stroke. He fell down the steps at his house. Our house. Where I'd lived with him on and off. I was supposed to come over that night. In Santa Fe. But I'd gone out with my friends for a drink. I didn't make it home that night. I fell asleep at my friend Mike's house up the road. Passed out. Drunk as a skunk again."

I sipped the tea, wished for a smoke so badly. I told him more. "I'd got into a fight with my girlfriend and was staying with Dad for a week or two, while we worked out what to do. Dad. Dad lived alone as usual, but he was fine, a fit sixty year old, that army training kept him doing well. It was just, he tripped. He fell. A stroke knocked him out. And he smashed his head on the stone steps at the front door." I took a deep breath. "I didn't make it home. Not that night. Not until the next day, lunchtime. I'd missed work, felt too hung-over. I couldn't do it. I wandered back to Dad's for a shower, to clean up, lie in front of cable. That kind of thing."

Frank moved around in his chair, settling back to watch me, not reaching for me this time. He knew better. The camera sat near him. I looked up at him with such sad eyes. He took the camera in his shaking hands and pointed it at me. *Click.* Me? Like this? I shook my head. I had more to tell.

"I walked up the street, it was chilly, October, and you know how that can be? Well, in New Mexico, it had threatened to snow, even then. That day, though, it was chilly but not bad. I liked walking home in the fresh crisp air. I opened the gate and saw him, lying there on the steps. I was mad at him, I remember thinking what had he done this time? I got to him and turned him over. His face was smashed up, blue and purple and swollen and his eyes rolled back. I couldn't tell if he was breathing. Unconscious. Then his eyes rolled back toward me. They were unfocused. He was gone. But shaking back and forth, his arms lashed at me. his body shivered. Frozen. His skin was cold to my touch. I screamed. I screamed. And he didn't hear me. He didn't hear me. He hasn't heard me since."

I broke down, sobbing, my head smashing against the table over and over until Frank's hands took me against him, holding me tightly, murmuring to me, words, sounds of his heart beating, and his chest, small and shaking as it was, held me solid. He kept me there, with me shaking, crying, and trying to—what, I didn't know. I broke down, telling him the rest.

I talked about the ambulance, the needles, the machines, the sirens, the police, and the ride to the Intensive Care Unit. I talked and talked to this stranger. Frank listened and held me. *My friend, my friend,* he kept saying as he stroked my head.

I finally said it: "If only I'd been there, if only I hadn't gone out drinking—"

25

I walked back to the Capitol and caught the bus to Willy Street. To the Crystal Corner Tavern, only a couple of blocks from where Chris and Michaela both lived. I sat at the long bar with the pool tables behind me. I didn't look the bartender in the eyes, just ordered a Jim Beam and a beer, Corona, no lime. I drank back the shot.

Then I went outside to smoke. A couple of older guys stood near me, talking about the football game. I couldn't make sense of the words. I heard them, but it was just background noise to the voices inside me. I turned up my collar and shivered. I fingered the camera in my pocket. The lights flickered above us. The snow kept falling. I watched a big family sedan come around the corner, slipping and sliding onto the side street. I saw a Prius slow down at the lights. Michaela. I stepped back into the bar and kept my back to the window. She didn't come in.

"You okay there?" The bartender wiped the glass in his hand.

"Rough day, but I'm okay. Thanks."

"Sure, no problem. I've seen you around, but not in here. You sure you're okay?"

I nodded and held out the empty shot glass with a smile. He took it and refilled it.

"On the house, hope the holidays aren't too bad for you." He nodded once and then walked away, off to serve a few students at the end of the bar near the jukebox.

I drank. I stepped out to smoke. I drank another. Or five.

Chris opened the door to me, her eyes widening as she saw me struggling to stand upright. She stepped close and smelled my breath, then let me have it.

"What the hell, Lucky? My folks are about to get here and you're drunk? What the hell are you doing?"

I wasn't in the mood. I pushed past her. I need a piss, I told her.

"Charming!" She watched me stumble in the hallway and into the bathroom. She came in after me and closed the door behind us.

"Are you okay? Did something happen?"

"No, I'm fine. Now, excuse me, but I need to piss." I waved loosely at the door. She stood there.

"Like I haven't seen it all before," she told me. "I'm going to run you a bath, okay? We have an hour before my folks get here, and we have to sober you up. We'll talk later, when they've gone to bed. We need to talk. But not now."

She leaned over and turned on the taps. I reached for her, wanting to kiss her.

"You have to be kidding! You think this is sexy? You stinking of cigarettes and booze? Stumbling and fumbling? Forget it, Lucky. You're not getting any."

Chris closed the curtains, and turned to me, appraising my state. She sighed and reached for my leather jacket, unzipping me.

"What happened to you, Lucky? You look terrible. Christ, you stink." Chris undressed me, slowly and cautiously. She sat me on the side of the tub, and took my boots off, and then pushed me backwards into the water. She opened the windows to let in some cold air.

"I'll get you some coffee." She assessed me as she left the door open. "Don't drown."

She walked down the hallway, calling out to Joanna that I was in the bathroom and to check on me for her. I heard footsteps. I looked up. I'd not seen Joanna angry before that. She stood in the doorway. Cold tension streamed off her, penetrating my foggy state.

"Are you really that much of an idiot, Lucky? With her parents coming to stay with us, and to meet you? Did you really just go get smashed? That's a new low."

"Fuck off. I had a bad day," I mumbled and gave her the finger.

She walked away, telling Chris that I had a weird sense of humor. They laughed over something or other and I heard the coffee machine gurgling. Chris brought me a huge steaming mug.

"I've thrown out your whiskey. The beers. too."

"Good." I looked up at her. "Thanks. I can't explain. But thanks, Chris." I looked away and sat in the tub, aware of her staring at me, but neither of us spoke. She closed the door behind her and I was alone. Wrecked, exhausted and alone.

"Mr. Wright. Mrs. Wright. Pleased to meet you."

I opened the front door when I heard the car pull up. Chris was in her room changing again. I took the parcels from her mom's arms and followed them into the living room. I'd gotten the fire going after my bath. I'd drunk more coffee. I'd never get any sleep tonight, at this rate. I took their coats, asking about their trip from Cleveland. Mr. Wright went into detail about the weather threatening to unleash the next big winter storm, but his wife stopped him with a laugh and a pat on the arm.

"That's enough, dear. Lucky was just being polite, weren't you? Coffee anyone?" The husband shrugged sheepishly and followed her into the kitchen. I was glad I'd cleaned up again. How Joanna and Chris made such a mess in a couple of hours, I had no idea.

I sat at the kitchen table with Mr. Wright. He asked about my family, work and my plans, basically trying to find out how long I was staying with his daughter. At that moment, Christine came in. I didn't have to answer. Neither his words nor her look.

I wandered back to the bathroom to wash my face in cold water again. I brushed my hair out of my eyes. I looked in the mirror. Yep, that was me, rough, drained and a mess. What a mess. I stood up, and tried to smile at myself. Joanna walked past, for once wearing a simple cotton dress and low heels, and she caught me watching.

"You ready?" She stopped in front of me, straightening out the material across her hips.

I turned and held my hands out to her. "I'm sorry for earlier."

She shrugged and said it was no big deal, for her, that is, but that I'd probably have to answer for it once the folks left on Friday. "But still, we're in this together until then. Let's go, huh?"

"I'm going out for a cigarette. Do you mind?" I asked Chris.

She glanced next door with a raised eyebrow.

"I'll be on the front porch. Not the side one," I told her, putting on my leather jacket.

She nodded slightly and carried on chatting to her mom about her brother's new girlfriend.

I stood outside, walking into the snow flurries, with my face turned up like Frank, trying to taste the flakes. I smoked slowly, not wanting to make more polite talk, and definitely not wanting to talk to Chris before we went to sleep in the same room. A first time in a week. I'd give her the sofa. I'd be sleeping on the rug in front of the fireplace. Could be worse.

26

I'd fallen asleep in the armchair, listening to *The Mirror Conspiracy* by Thievery Corporation. I stirred my aching legs, and stretched a few stiff muscles before I stood up. My jeans had killed a few nerves and I stumbled briefly before catching myself. I took off the black sweatshirt and tucked in the t-shirt. I looked over at Chris, saying nothing. I came over to her. She lay hidden under the sleeping bag and blankets, curled up in a tight ball.

"Go away, Lucky. I'm not talking to you."

"Okay. You don't have to talk." I sat on the carpet in front of where I thought her head might be. I pulled back the blankets to reveal her staring at me, eyes reddened and she pouted at me, like a little kid. I tucked in the blankets around her chin and then I settled in. I stroked the hair out of her eyes. I didn't say anything. Neither did she. I looked at her and she looked away, and then closed her eyes. I stroked her hair, her cheeks, wiping away the tears that kept falling. I tasted them, one by one.

"Why are you doing that?" she whispered.

"To take the pain away. I didn't want it soaking back in to you."

A shadow of a smile crept across her tired face. She opened her eyes. "Oh, Lucky, why are you such a pain? And so charming, too? You're driving me crazy."

I didn't know what to say to that. I smiled back at her, nervously. "You're still mad at me?"

"Yes."

"Oh."

"But it's okay. Something happened today, didn't it?"

"Yes, but right now, it's you I want to talk about. What's making you cry, sweetheart? It's not me, is it? Getting drunk like that?"

"Well, it sure didn't help." She sighed and untucked herself a bit from all the bedding and she sat up. I stayed on the rug at her feet, looking up at her, until she patted the cushion next to her. I moved up. We sat there for some time before Chris turned to me, all young and innocent in her striped pajamas. "My mom. She likes you, she told me."

"Really? And that made you cry?" I joked.

"No, but she so desperately wants me to settle down, get a job, stop being a student. Why can't I be more like Joanna and work with children? Be a teacher? Be a mom? I'm not going to. Why doesn't she understand me?" and she cried, burying her head into my shoulder. I held her. Nothing I could say. I've had no experience with moms. Not really. Chris cried into my t-shirt. I just held her tightly to me.

She sat back after a while, not looking at me, but settling against me, as we stared at the fire. I leaned forward and poked it again, brushing the ashes to the side.

"Dad's okay," she said after a while. "It's simple with him, he wants me and my brother to be happy, nothing more or less. He doesn't care how we do it, or who we choose, but just to find someone we like, and find good work, a good community to live in. That kind of thing. A simple man. He liked you, I think."

"Not sure?"

"He didn't say in so many words, but the fact that he talked to you about his work at the store and even asked about the gallery show. Yeah, I'd say he liked you. So far."

"Thanks for the vote of confidence, Chris!" I teased.

She smiled and took my hand. "What are we going to do?"

"I don't know. I honestly don't know, sweetheart."

"You've never called me that before tonight."

I held her hand in mine, searching out the scars and flaws we all have, the stories locked away in our bodies. "No?"

"No." She took her hand from mine and took my face, making me turn to her, direct. "What are we going to do, Lucky? Do you want to stay with me?"

I kept my eyes on hers. "I need to talk to you. Tell you what's going on." She flinched. She let her hands fall to her sides. I sat back and stared into the fire. I told her. I told her about Dad. About Mike. And about my day, of how I met Frank and what happened when I was there. I told her. No more secrets.

Well, none that came to mind.

27

"I'm leaving."

"Oh, really?" she asked with an eyebrow raised, leaning in for a light. We stood on her porch out back, under the eaves and out of the storm. "When? And where has your young lady gone this morning?"

I put the matches away and sighed. "She's taken her parents to the local homeless shelter to help out. Good Christians. They do their bit."

"Sarcasm?"

"Yeah. How did you guess?"

She took her hands out of the thick wool coat, tucked her hair into her hat, and pulled me closer. "Come here, Lucky, and tell me more."

I sighed again. She didn't know what had been going on. We'd seen each other in the street, waved as she drove past me and Chris walking hand in hand. But no, we hadn't talked; flirtatious text messages didn't count for conversation. Do they ever?

"I have a bit of an attitude toward people who tell me what I can and can't do," I muttered.

She laughed and held me closer. "I've noticed. But what's your problem with them specifically?"

I told her about how they affect Chris. Talking about Chris was easier these days. Michaela knew not to mention her own lover, though. We chatted about how parents have all these expectations, to live on through their kids. That kind of thing. I didn't get it.

"Dad just wanted me out of his hair. Too much work for a lone army officer. He tried to get me join up, but they rejected me! You should've seen his face when the letter came. Funny shit."

"What did he do?"

"He took me out to get drunk with him, and then told me to move out the next day. '*No child of mine,* etc, etc.'" I shivered at the memory. "At least I'd been seventeen by then. Not so bad an age to go out and make it in the world, right? Where's your family? Aren't you going to introduce me to them?"

"I hadn't planned on it, no." She'd smiled at me as she said that. Damn, Michaela was honest. It took some getting used to. She looked up the road. "How much time do we have?"

"For what?"

"To get Lucky, so to speak."

I turned beet-red and looked at the time on my phone. "Enough. But where's everyone?"

"Out. Shopping." She untangled herself from my leather jacket and stroked my cheek. "Well?"

I looked up the road, didn't see anyone, and followed her inside, shutting the door rapidly. Scared. Addicted. I put the phone on vibrate and followed Michaela up the by now familiar steps to her bedroom.

I shut the curtains. She opened them, shaking her head at me. She pulled me into the middle of the room, out of sight of the house next door. She took off my coat and found my camera. She laid it on the table next to the bed. She touched my green denim shirt, stroking the soft cotton lightly. I moved toward her.

"No, this time you let me, Lucky. No questions, okay? Allow me." With that, she smiled widely, wickedly, and slid my shirt off me. "I take what I want of you, for once. And you'll give it up. Willingly, right?"

I nodded.

She unbuckled my belt, undid my jeans and stepped back, looking me up and down. She reached for my camera. I stepped forward, to take it back, but she shook her finger at me, and turned it on. The camera.

"Let's see how it feels for you. What do you think? Can you take it, Lucky?"

And she took a photo of me standing there, hand outstretched. "Undress for me. For the camera, Lucky."

I shook my head. I can't, I told her.

"Oh yes, you can. You will."

And she walked around me, taking shot after shot. I slowly began to undress, dropping the jeans, and soon enough I was standing there as naked as can be, with my lover coming closer and stepping away whenever I made to touch her. She sat me down on the bed, talking as she went, standing over me, clicking away. I couldn't look into the lens, until she tapped me on the head.

"Lucky?"

I looked up. She took another photo, a close up, of my confusion, the lust, and the fear. She dropped the camera on the bed behind me. She took what she wanted and left the rest.

28

"I'm leaving."

Christine lowered her fork. Her mom passed the gravy to Joanna.

"Oh, really?" Chris asked, staring at me. "When?"

I put my knife and fork down, reaching for the glass of water—that's all I was drinking. "On Saturday. I might get an Amtrak ticket from Chicago to Lamy in New Mexico. It only takes 24 hours. A day trip, practically. Or maybe take the Nissan. I'm not sure. I'll work it out later."

"Oh, that's wonderful, Lucky." Her mom looked up with a wide smile. "If you go by train, we can take you to the station, can't we, Dad? It'll be a day later than we thought, but that's fine with you, isn't it, dear? Maybe we'll just stay an extra night, whatever you chose to do! That's all right, isn't it?"

Chris looked back and forth from one parent to the other. She didn't say anything, just started to eat again, sipping from the red wine she and Joanna were sharing. She drained her glass before asking why now, why was I leaving now? However, she didn't ask what I'd been doing all morning. Sitting at the table, the camera pushed against my thigh. A silent guilt trip. Nervously, I talked. I told them all about how my dad was in the hospital and I needed to go visit him again, to see if there was any change.

"God willing, he'll be where he needs to be." Her dad sat back, his plate empty and shaking his head when offered more. He sipped his cold beer. I craved some, myself. I sipped the water again.

"Which is where?"

"It's in His hands, Lucky. Don't you believe that? What church did you say you were raised in?"

"The church of the U.S. Army."

Chris kicked me under the table. Joanna choked and then kicked me, too. I looked at them both, a frown building.

"We didn't have a church," I explained. "I grew up all over the place. No religious experiences for me."

Her mom shook her head, sadly. "I'm sorry to hear that, and about your father, Lucky. But yes, it's in God's hands now, isn't it?"

"The doctors,' more likely."

"Well, they work for God."

There was a short silence. I stared at the table, plates of broccoli, potatoes, sweet potatoes, stuffing, cranberries, gravy, ham and turkey. Too much for us to eat. My stomach turned, just thinking of my dad living off intravenously dripped 'food.' Sickened by the sight of the feast before us.

"The doctors tell me what to do. I haven't talked to them recently, admittedly. But it's up to them." I repeated.

Chris stood, and took the empty plate from her dad. I turned away and didn't catch her eyes asking me to follow her. She said it anyway. "Can you help me in the kitchen, Lucky?"

I stood up, a teenager in trouble. I picked up my own plate. "Sure." Sullen.

"Anyone want coffee? We'll make some for all of us. Give us a moment." Chris didn't wait for an answer, she just pushed me into the kitchen, closing the door behind us. I put the plate in the sink and started to run the hot water to fill the basin. Chris reached past me and turned off the tap.

"Not now. What's going on, Lucky? Why are you picking a fight with my dad? I thought you liked him." She leaned back against the counter, and then punched me lightly on the arm. "Hey, it's me, your friend. Talk to me, Lucky. What's up?"

"Shouldn't we put the coffee on?"

She started to fix the machine. "That doesn't get you off the hook, but yes, a full pot of coffee. So what's up with the comments about the doctors?"

"I started thinking last night, after you fell back asleep, about Dad. In the intensive care unit at the hospital. I got online and started reading about strokes, and most of it talked about the rehab and all of that." I paused as she ran the water into the pot. "All of that stuff is irrelevant for him. Us. And it took me ages to find anything about people like Dad. The proper names for it. I didn't remember what the doctors had told me, the prognosis, or whatever the right word is. So I had to keep looking."

I ran the water to wash the dishes. Chris didn't stop me this time. "I finally found sites about traumatic brain injuries. That was the only place where I got descriptions that matched what I remembered. And it was mostly ethical discussions by Christians, talking about the papal decree not to let them die, and how since man was an image of God, we can't kill them in the name of science or God. Fucking joke, right? How many wars are there in the name of God?"

My hands shook underwater, staying busy with washing and wiping the plates. Chris stood nearby but said nothing.

I carried on. "I read about how there is a whole political religious movement to prevent doctors from letting people like my dad die."

"What's wrong with him? You told me about the stroke, but how bad is it?"

I laughed. A bitter harsh sound, even for me. "P.V.S. A persistent vegetative state."

"Oh, Christ."

I laughed at that. "Yes, and that's my problem today. With Christ. Or rather with the Pope. Telling me what I can and can't do for Dad."

I turned and looked at her, the helpless rage etched in the lines around my eyes. I stood there, saying nothing.

"Is everything all right, dear?" Chris turned at her mom's question as she opened the door and came in with more dirty plates. She handed them to me and I busied myself, not looking up as the two of them took the coffee fixings back in with them.

"Take your time," whispered Chris as she passed me, carrying a tray of cups and saucers.

"Why now?"

"It's your fault." I smiled weakly. She sat back on the swing. We'd come for a walk to what I thought of as our park. The lake was partially iced over and silently welcoming in a strange way. I pushed the swing. I took another shot of her, a pensive expression this time, not the light freedom of our first afternoon together. She turned at the sound of the camera and sighed.

"Can't you do anything without taking a photograph?"

I put it away, thinking of how I'd have to be careful now. I couldn't let her find out about my morning with Michaela. I smiled at her again and pushed the swing harder. She laughed and jumped off.

"Come on, seriously, Lucky. Why do you want to go see him now? Why are you thinking about him now?" She held out her hand for mine and we started to walk down the street, the one parallel to the lakeside. "I know we talked the other night, well, last night, but I don't get what made you change your mind."

"It's like I said. Talking to you. Talking to Michaela. Seeing you and your families made me—"

"You've seen her?" Chris interrupted me.

"Yes," I admitted but I didn't elaborate. "Families. Holidays. Talking to Frank yesterday. It's that time, isn't it? I didn't want him to, but Dad kept creeping into my head, the image of him hooked up to those machines. I'm surrounded by the memories. The sounds of the machines constantly beeping in time with the rise and fall of his chest. The nurses patting me on the shoulder as they moved him, turned him every few hours. The doctors would talk to me when they did tests. I had so many questions. No answers. Time will tell. That's what they told me, over and over. I got sick of it. No changes. Pneumonia for a week, then his lungs cleared up. But nothing else. He just can't do anything. I don't even know if he can hear me. I held his hand and watched him breathe."

"He's on a machine for that, too?"

"Yes. But they thought he could do it for himself. After that scare with the pneumonia, they took him off it. And he held his ground for a couple of days, but then he got worse again. I know the sound of his breath, the rattle that comes and goes. Have you ever listened to your dad's heart?"

I looked over at Christine, walking at my side. Who was this woman? Ten years younger than me, she'd never lost anyone, no friends or family or even pets. An innocent. How could she possibly understand?

The driveways were piled with the snowfall of the last twenty-four hours. Snowmen with scarves and carrot noses lined the streets. A thin fresh layer of snow covered the cars. I shivered slightly and zipped up. The camera reminded me again of its sins. I strode on, picking up the pace. Chris kept holding on to me, uncomplaining even as she slipped once or twice. I pulled out the cigarettes.

"Do you mind?"

She shook her head and let go of my hand as I fumbled in the cold to light the smoke I craved so desperately. We walked for another hour, turning back to the idea of my leaving. She talked about how hard it is to be around her mom and dad for more than two days at a time, but that it'd make sense for me to stay until the weekend. Easy for all of us, especially for her, it's help to have company with her parents around. She didn't ask if I was planning on coming back. Or when. We kept it vague. The logistics. The exams she had the first week in December. And the show. The show, I'd forgotten about the show.

"I'll need to talk to John about that," I said. "Maybe I'll go over in the morning and talk to him. Let him know."

"I hope he doesn't cancel the show if you're not here. What will you tell him?" We turned into her driveway. I glanced up at Michaela's window and then back to Christine as she pulled out her house key.

"The truth," I answered righteously.

29

I did, too. I told him the truth.

We sat at the desk in his office at the back of the house. The window overlooked Christine's bedroom on the ground floor and her curtains were open, with the shadowy figures of her parents moving around inside. Vague. I was glad to notice it was hard to make out the details. Not used to living in such close quarters, I'd forgotten why people had curtains. Must remember. Must remember to close the damn curtains.

"Let's see. Since you're leaving tomorrow, we'll need to set up phone interviews. Would that work for you, Lucky?" John looked up from his computer to make a note of something on the pad next to it. He glanced at me. "Yes? Did you have a question?" He smoothed down his tie and tucked it into the jacket.

Did he always dress so tidily? I became conscious of my old blue jeans and torn shirtsleeves. I put my hands on my knees, out of sight, clearing my throat. "Do I have to do interviews? Can't you just give them a press release or something?"

He smiled. "More comfortable behind the lens and not in front?"

The heat flashed across my neck. I scratched my head. He didn't notice. Or at least, he made no comment. He continued by explaining how the press release works to generate interest but doesn't make for a story, a newspaper article.

"And that's what we want. A story, one about the archetypal journey your work embodies. Do you have new photos to show us or would you rather we stick to what you've shown?"

"What you have, if that's okay?" I kept myself from reaching to pat the camera. I couldn't show those last images to anyone. I could barely look at them myself. The shame and longing that was burning in my eyes in each of those photos. I had no pride for what happened. I should just delete them, I'd thought, but I didn't. I couldn't.

John offered me a cup of tea while we worked out the details. The media. The angle he wanted us to promote. He said, though, that it was up to me for the interviews to come across. He would prompt the journalist as to what made this fascinating on paper and more so, in person with the images on the walls.

"Captions? Do you have any?"

I shook my head. "Not all of them. I had a few worked out. I could email them to you if you like."

He wrote down the address on the back of a business card and stretched across the desk to hand it to me. I pocketed it, touching the camera quickly. He sat back. He asked about the releases. "Do you need help getting in touch with some of these people?"

"What do you mean?"

"I can send out a basic form to people, like this Daniel, or the girls in the diner, and have them sign and return them. It's less for you to do before you leave."

"Sounds good, yes, thanks." I drank some of the tea, black, strong, just as Frank Walker made his tea. Ah, Frank, I needed to visit him. "Could I print up something new? It'd just take a moment." I told him about my chance encounter with Frank and the portraits I'd taken. And how I'd promised to bring him a copy of each one.

John stood up; make yourself at home, he offered. "I'll let you work it out while I make some phone calls to a few friends at the papers. See if anyone is working today. Probably not but it's worth a try, you know?"

I hooked up the camera, hoping to hell that no one came in. Neither John, nor Michaela. I couldn't face her. I didn't want to look into her eyes or feel her touch on my skin. Too much. She was too much for me. I knew it but still I wanted more.

I found the images of Frank. I printed the one of him under the streetlamp, and another of him at his kitchen table. I'd forgotten the one he'd taken of me and on the spur of the moment, I printed that one, too. The haunted look in my eyes stunned me. Was that what people saw?

I closed the file, checked that nothing had downloaded that I didn't want John to see, and then I found him in the kitchen with his family. The parents, the teenage kids and his sister, that is—my lover, Michaela. They all looked up at me and smiled, saying hello. John introduced me as his new protégé. I showed him the new photos and he nodded encouragingly. He passed them around. They each shook my hand, warm greetings, smiles at the images, and offers of fresh brewed coffee.

I avoided looking at Michaela too much. She stood up from her corner at the table, and passed me a mug of hot coffee, black with no sugar, just how I like it. She smiled and touched my arm briefly on her way out, saying to the rest of them that she was going out for a cigarette. Groans from the kids.

"Don't you smoke?" asked John. "Isn't that how you two met?"

I nodded and sipped my drink. Jim Beam always made it taste better. I'd have to get used to it straight up. I sighed. "Yeah, do you mind if I go out, too?"

"No, I did get hold of a reporter, Angela—she wants to come over and talk to you in person before you leave. Shall I call her back? Tell her to come over in the next hour if she can? And I think we should offer her this portrait of you. It's striking. Disturbingly honest."

"Sure." Thinking 'Oh, shit' but agreeing, nonetheless. I put the leather back on and stepped out to join Michaela. She moved aside, making space under the porch. We looked over to Christine's house at the same time, then caught each other, and laughed. I leaned back against the wall out of sight.

She lit my cigarette. I smoked, sipped my coffee. I had nothing to say. Or was it too much to say? What's the difference? She touched me lightly on the cheek. That tenderness became my undoing once again, and my eyes teared up. She shook her head softly. She stood there, close to me, and then walked back inside alone.

30

"I'm leaving."

Frank opened the door even wider in surprise and ushered me back into the kitchen. I'd brought with me a bag of treats from Christine's. He was wearing a loose pair of brown corduroy pants and a white shirt, tucked in to the high waist. He pushed his hand through his wispy hair as he sat down. The metal table was clear but for some letters opened and lying to the side of him. I handed the photos to him as soon as I put the teakettle on to boil. The kitchen was tidy but cluttered. I offered the brown bag. The rest of the goodies.

"What's this?" Frank opened it and started to pull out some shortbread cookies, some organic milk, a container of chicken noodle soup, and a box of PG Tips. "Really? Are you sure? That's awfully thoughtful of you, Lucky."

I admitted that it all came from Chris and the family. They wanted me to bring him over for dinner that night, so he could spend some time with us all before I left. He loved the idea and worried about what to wear, and how cold was it outside. Personally, I thought Chris needed a buffer between herself and the parents and that's why she sent me off so willingly. I was told to come back my five; dinner would be ready at six. I was over the God shit, even though they didn't push it on me once we stopped talking about Dad, but still, I couldn't fake it much longer.

I'd been taking time off from the family all afternoon to work on captions, by researching the basic progression of mythical journeys. Did my photos match up with the steps in such a tale? It was fascinating, to be honest. I wanted to call the show *Sex, Death and Photography*. Not sure if James and John would find that appropriate. Maybe. Maybe, I could explain why that title spoke to me. I'd have to ask. Simple as that.

As I passed the prints to Frank, I thought of how I'd like to add them to the show. But none of the others. Yeah, he was a presence. One that I wanted to acknowledge. Frank held each of the three photos, closely examining each before laying them on the table between us.

"Do I really look that old? And defenseless? How strange! I don't feel it!" He smiled up at me when I stood to pour the water into the teapot. He opened the box of shortbread and I passed him a plate to put them on. The sun warmed the room, with the broad window capturing all the afternoon's sunshine or clouds. A Weather Channel if ever I saw one.

"This reminds me of New Mexico. The reds and yellows, blues and greens of all you have in here. The huge window. The heat on me. I miss the open skies."

Frank shook his head, "Yes, today is a good day here. On the gray days, though, not so enlightening, shall we say? What a gloomy room this is then. It all depends." He ate a cookie before asking me about my plans.

"Well," I looked around again, not sure where to begin. I told him about getting drunk after I'd left him and how mad Christine had been with me. That is, until she heard the whole story.

"Seeing you, well, meeting you, and then being around Chris and her parents, and visiting my other friend Michaela and her family, I couldn't stop thinking abut my Dad. I remembered it all. And how I left after the break-up with my girlfriend. I didn't see any point in staying there just for Dad. He didn't know I existed. He didn't know *he* existed," I said with a wry smile.

Frank nodded at me, knowing. He poured the tea for us both.

"But later that night, I thought about Dad. I couldn't sleep so I did some research online about Dad. Strokes. Brain injuries. And it made me realize I needed to see him. Who else did he have? No one. Someone needed to talk to the doctors on his behalf."

"In what way? I mean, I have an advocate here, someone who comes with me when I see the doctor for all my aches and pains. Nothing serious, luckily. But your Dad? What's he like now? Can he walk or talk yet? That seems to come back slowly, from what I've seen of friends of mine."

I shook my head. "He's basically in a coma. That's not the right word for it. And I still haven't spoken to a doctor directly, nor the neurosurgeon. I talked to the head nurse and she told me that he's maintained. But. No changes to speak of. Sometimes he reacts to sound, pressure or pain. But no comprehension. He's gone." I looked down, unable to face the concern in Frank's eyes.

"That's terrible, Lucky. I worry about that for myself. Quality of life."

"I know. That's what I'm thinking about. If he has some responses, it gives me hope. Maybe someone's still in there? I need to find out. One way or the other, I need to find out. I want to talk to him, hold his hand, watch the monitors and see if there is a reaction when I talk to him about what he wants. I wouldn't want that for me, either. Stuck inside a body and not be able to do anything. Say anything. How could it be better than dying? Who for?" I finally looked up, struggling to talk and drink tea as if this was the most normal of conversations.

"What were his beliefs?" asked Frank.

I blew on the tea and took a gulp. "Dad and I never talked about much, just books, dinner, television shows, and the latest NFL game, of course! We kept it simple. What about you? Have you thought about this stuff?"

"I have a living will. Do you?"

I shook my head, not knowing what he was talking about. He explained that it meant he had a 'Do Not Resuscitate' order. So he wouldn't be kept alive in times like those Dad was living through. "Does he have one?"

"No idea. We never talked about it. Death. After Mom died in that car crash when I was a kid, after the funeral, we sort of avoided the topic, you know? Not a happy one for us. So we played football, went skating, hiked in the hills or along beaches, depending on what base he was stationed at. It changed every few years."

Frank sat back with another cookie and talked about his own time in the Forces, the travels and the foreign girls, the village bars and the incredible fear that struck him when war was declared. He'd been in his twenties. He ended up on tour in Greece. Met his wife and against the orders of the officers and without the family approval, they'd been married. Two kids. Grandkids. Forty-six years together. All his remaining family now lived in Europe or on the West Coast these days. He was in Madison alone.

"Want to see some photographs?" And then he laughed, "What am I thinking! Of course you do! You probably can't get enough, can you?" He stood up, put his hand on my shoulder as he walked past. "You just wait there, my friend. I'll find the little suitcase I keep beside my bed." He tapped me lightly and affectionately, humming to himself.

31

Chris left the room to open the front door. The dinner was simmering in the kitchen and the fire kept the living room toasty. It was my last night in town. I'd packed my bags and stored them in the hallway. Everything had gone pretty smoothly. Frank and Chris's dad were chatting away about politics. I heard the door open but then Joanna waved me into the kitchen, closing the door behind us.

"It's Michaela. I saw her cross the garden. What the hell have you done now, Lucky?"

I laughed out loud, nervously. "Nothing! Honest! I haven't seen her since yesterday morning." I realized my mistake as soon as the words came out.

Joanna stood still. She stared at me. "Oh, no. You didn't?"

I leaned against the counter. "Please, no. Don't tell her, Joanna. Please!"

Her skirt matched the fabric of the curtains. I didn't point it out to her. My hands stretched out to her, my eyes begging, but she didn't respond. I looked around the room, and went to sit down at the table, grabbing a beer from the fridge on my way. Joanna watched me, her brown eyes blaming me, shaming me. She finally turned back to the kitchen door. "Let's see what the professor has to say."

I drank back half the pilsner as fast as I could and followed her. They all turned to us as we came in.

"Joanna, this is Michaela, my English teacher. I was just explaining to my parents and to Frank here, that we've lived next door but had never socialized before. And since it's still Thanksgiving, and

Lucky knows her so well, I wanted us all together for an evening." Christine babbled, talking fast as she took a drink to Michaela, who had dressed in her tight black pants and a short dark green shirt that emphasized her long tall frame. Her hair was loose, held behind her ears, and a with a hint of lipstick, she smiled at me when Chris announced, "Dinner will be in ten minutes so if you two want to smoke, now is the time."

Christine ushered us both out the back door and onto the porch steps. I heard her talking quietly to Joanna as the door closed us outside. Michaela and I looked at each other, and then laughed.

"What the hell?" came out of one of us—or both of us, probably. I pulled out my tobacco and lighter, dropping it into the snow at the bottom of the steps. I went to find it but slipped, face forward into the drift piled up at the side. Michaela grabbed me by the scruff of the neck, and laughingly repeated her original line, "Steady on your feet, Sailor!"

She dusted me off and handed my back my lighter.

"Well, this is an appropriate end to your visit, isn't it, Lucky? A full cycle, nice and complete?" She leaned into me, quickly kissing me deeply. "I was quite surprised by the invitation, but I couldn't say no. Too fascinating! I want to see how this plays out. What do you think Chris wants from us?"

"I don't know. But she doesn't know about yesterday. Please don't say anything, okay?"

"What do you think I am? Of course I wouldn't say anything, Lucky. Don't worry."

I took a deep breath and told her that I just let it slip with Joanna. I had no idea what to expect. What she'd do.

"Ah, well, this will be most interesting." She touched me lightly on the arm. "Don't worry, Lucky. It's going to be fine. Let's go in, shall we?"

32

"Pass the pepper, will you, Lucky?"

I did as told, hardly looking anyone in the eyes. I simply sat at the table as Chris seated everyone according to some plan. The conversations flowed surprisingly easily. One of Adele's CDs played quietly in the background.

Both Michaela and Christine were turning on the charm with Frank and the parents, talking about literature over the ages. Frank had studied the Greek Philosophers and talked in detail about Joseph Campbell's work bringing myths into the general public attention. He'd heard him speak one year, up in Minnesota, at the student theater in St. Paul. Michaela sat forward and then the two of them went off, in great detail, about the power of knowing these stories, not just history alone.

I sat back and began to relax. I caught Christine's eye and she smiled innocently. A little unnerving but I went with it and passed her the salt, too. She had seated herself and Michaela opposite me, with Joanna to my left, Frank to my right, and the parents at each end of the dining table. The candles flickered and I glanced over to the fire, thinking to poke it, to get some bigger flames. But I sensed Chris watching me, shaking her head at me, reading me so clearly.

I smiled slightly and took the beer—only my third—and I took a sip. I'd slowed down once I saw how well behaved everyone was. The parents had no clue. Heads turning back and forth, they were trying to keep up, adding their own stories about families and books, and simply enjoying the new people. Frank's face was flushed. I hoped it wasn't too much for him. I listened in. I finished my roast chicken and potatoes. The good mid-western supper went down well, especially knowing I'd soon be home in the land of enchiladas and red chile. I couldn't wait to get back there. For the food.

"What are the stages?"

I tuned back to find everyone looking at me. "Huh?"

"The main stages to the Hero's journey. What are they?" Michaela asked me, tying her hair up in a tight bun.

I looked at Frank. "Help me out here! You know this stuff better than me!"

He toasted me with his glass of red wine. "She is a teacher, after all. What did you expect? I would think this is a chance to see how much you've learned about the Journey since that is apparently the theme of the photography show, isn't it?" He nodded at Michaela, to her delight. They touched glasses and turned to me.

"Oh, right. Hmm. Well, from what I can gather, I'm sort of recreating the myth of crisis, or conflict that sends me out of the nest and into the big world. The photos deal with loss, love, betrayal, finding faith and facing death. I guess it's a crisis that forces the departure, and hopefully that's followed by a sense of fulfillment, coming from reaching some goal or challenge, oh, and then there's the return. And when you consider that I'm about to go back to New Mexico, it's all part of it, right? Does that cover it?" I sat back.

They both nodded in encouragement. And they waited for more. I leaned forward again and tried to articulate what comes more easily through images. I wanted to reach for the camera, to capture the expressions as I talked about the way the hospital destroyed me, and the time here had opened me back up.

Chris watched me, her frown slowly fading. Joanna, on the other hand, avoided my eyes. She stood and left the room, closing the door softly behind her. I focused back on the conversation around me.

"Do you feel that the story is complete?" Mr. Wright asked me.

"No. Not at all. And that's what's confusing to me as I try to write the captions for the photographs. It's as if I'm ending something, trying to contain something that has only just begun. There's more to come."

Michaela explained that that is exactly the process. "If you read tarot," she said, "you'd know how each part of our lives has phases. A good response to the work being done doesn't mean completion. It's just another stage. It never ends. More challenges will come soon enough!"

I sighed and everyone laughed. "Okay, okay, I know. Life's not easy. Well. Anyway, what's for dessert? Or do I have to go make it myself?"

The coffee mellowed us all out after we ate the homemade apple pie, a surprise offering from Mrs. Wright. We all relaxed in various armchairs, sofas, and across the cushions on the rug in front of the fire. I brushed some ash onto my palm and tossed it into the flames. I leaned back against the sofa, with Christine's legs touching my back. She didn't move away from me. Frank had nodded off. We all smiled as he softly snored.

"I can drive him home in bit," offered Michaela. She stood, gesturing to the cigarette in her hand, with a shrug and smile. "It's that time."

She went out and Joanna followed her. Strange. Chris and I looked up at each other with concern. For different reasons. We talked quietly about the plans for the next day. I'd have to get up earlier than I was used to, but Chris said she'd take us all to Joanna's workplace for breakfast.

"Seems appropriate since that's where we met!" and she poked me gently in the arm. "We can talk about population studies like before, and then you carry on with your Journey as if you hadn't stayed." Her voice betrayed a bittersweet sadness. I stroked her foot. She moved it away.

Joanna and Michaela walked back in, shaking off the flurries that covered their jackets.

"It's coming down again. I think we should get Frank home in a minute. I'd prefer to go before it settles on the roads. I don't like the idea of getting stuck on my way home alone."

"Why don't you go with her, Lucky? You can make sure she gets home safely," suggested Joanna.

I looked up sharply at her. And then to Chris. She nodded tiredly, her eyes blank and colder than before as she looked between the three of us.

"You don't have to come with me, Lucky. I know how you like to clean up so why don't you stay?" Michaela teased, but Mr. and Mrs. Wright were already up and taking the cups and saucers away, bustling around, telling us they were off to bed once they'd done the dishes. Chris waved my concerns off and told me to wake Frank and take him home.

"I'll see you later."

I had no choice. Joanna passed me my leather and smiled sweetly. "Don't forget your camera, Lucky."

33

"Are you going to stay in touch with us?"

Michaela pulled out of the driveway onto Williamson, heading us into town with Frank. She took a quick glance at me in her mirror as Frank was looking out of the window at the stores and the snowflakes.

"Yes, I'd say so. Don't you think so, Frank? We'll meet again, right?"

"Oh yes. In the New Year, I'll come over to the show. You'll have to remind me. I might forget." He turned to face me in the backseat, thanking me for a wonderful night. He made me promise to write a letter, a real letter, once I knew how my Dad was.

Michaela looked at me sharply, a question mark in her eyes. I shook my head. Later, I mouthed to her. We drove the two miles taking it slowly. The roads were empty, snow-packed, and unplowed as yet. I stared out the window, thinking of winter in Santa Fe, wondering if this was one of the wet snowy winters or were we having another drought? I had no idea. I hadn't kept up. But I would be leaving in the morning, driving for days, and returning home to face what needed to be done for my Dad, however long it took. If I didn't get back in time for the show, too bad.

Bundled up in his long army winter coat, Frank hugged me once we got to his place, and then he gave me a photo of himself at my age, living in England with his family. Thick trees, sheep, dogs, and rising hills in the background of the farmhouse. His kids grinned toothlessly at the camera. A beautiful moment.

"Family." He said nothing else.

"Are you going to stay in touch with me, too?" Michaela asked as we drove away.

"Yeah. Email or phone calls?"

"For me, emails. I'll say more. But don't expect me to be waiting for you, Lucky."

"What do you mean?"

"You're a romantic. A troubled romantic. I am more of a free spirit. But you know that, don't you?" She took the smoke from my hand and flicked the ash out of the window. "I can't give you what you need. Do I need to spell it out for you?"

"Yes, I guess so."

She sighed and opened the window wider, taking a short detour to the park. We parked next it, watching the full moon fill the horizon.

"I'm telling you that Christine is who you need to focus on. She's good. A good person. And good for you, by the looks of it. She loves you, can't you tell?"

"She does?" I stared out of the window, past the swings I knew so well. Does she? I asked myself. Is that what's going on? I shrugged, leaned back in the seat. "But what about sex? With you—"

"Don't compare your lovers. You know better than that, Lucky! What we do, did, it's powerful, a gift. But it burns out too fast. It's not something to build a life around. I like to be able to do what I want when I want. I have a full life on my own. I don't want more. You do. I see you as needing a home, hoping to settle down with someone. Chris could be that someone, you know? Anyway, I like her. I liked being there tonight."

"But, Michaela, with you, I come apart."

She watched me closely. "And she'll rebuild you. And you'll give her the strength to follow what she needs for herself, and not the dreams of her parents. You're leaving tomorrow to take care of your Dad. I don't know the story. I don't need to. But I know I'll see you again. Keep the photos to remember me. This. Promise?"

I nodded and reached for her, but she turned her cheek to me. I kissed her softly, sadly.

Michaela started the engine and drove us home.

34

The house was silent. I crept into the living room to find one candle still burning. On the sofa lay Chris, half bundled up in her blankets and pajamas. I took my leather off, exhausted. It had been a draining few days. I sat down to take my boots and socks off. I couldn't tell if she was awake or not. I put another two logs on the fire. I sat back and stared at it. Leaving in the morning. What a concept.

Chris stirred. A little voice asked if I'd had a good evening. And had Frank enjoyed himself?

I told her about the conversation with Michaela about the two of us. That we're good for each other. Is that what she thought? I asked.

Silence greeted me. I looked over finally to find her facing me. Her big blue eyes teared up. Her hair was sticking out in all direction and her pajama top was misbuttoned. She didn't say anything.

We stared at each other. Neither of us moved. Then I stood and came to her. I took off my sweatshirt and t-shirt. I dropped my jeans on the floor. I pulled back her blankets carefully. I lay down next to her, and wrapped myself around her.

No words were spoken. She curled up into me, nestling against my chest, her arms up and around my neck and shoulders. I lay still. I did no more. Skin to skin. Breathing in time. We fell asleep.

At some point in the night we woke, and the embers still glowed. Outside I watched the snow falling in the lamplight. I turned to her as she did to me.

"It's not too late," I whispered to her. "It's not too late."

35

I panicked. I searched my bags once again. The parents were hugging Chris goodbye in the parking lot outside. I had hidden myself in the bathroom at the diner. I desperately searched again and again, each and every pocket of the backpack. I tipped out the clothes from the black duffel bag. Not there. It wasn't there. The bathroom closed in on me and I found myself unable to breathe properly. I started to panic. I sat down on the floor among all my crap, my notes and shorts and tees and computer and—no camera. Nowhere. No camera. What the hell?

I'd packed the day before. I'd put it all in the bags in the hallway and left them there. What could have happened? Then Joanna's voice came back to me. Last night, as I was about to leave with Michaela, she'd told me, "Don't forget your camera, Lucky."

What the hell? I threw everything back in to the bags, and stood up shakily. The green walls and dirty floor assaulted my eyes and suddenly I was sick to my stomach. Did you know that puking out your nose burns? I didn't until that morning. That morning at the damn diner where Joanna worked. Where this all started.

"My camera. Where is it?" I spat out the question, cornering her by the front door as Chris started walking back in. Joanna pushed me off her.

"I don't know what you mean." With that she opened the door to her roommate and then walked outside, joining her arm in arm. I followed them out with my bags. I stood next to the Lexus, and shook in rage. In fear. What the hell? I walked over to my truck and threw in the bag and started the engine. I got back out, wondering what to do. Chris came up to me. She hugged me and suddenly looked up at me.

"Are you okay? You're trembling, Lucky. Are you cold?"

"No, I don't know. Didn't sleep too well," I joked and kissed her when her parents weren't looking. They were saying goodbye to Joanna. I turned to Christine.

"I'll call you, talk to you as soon as I know something. Give me a few days, all right? Trust me. Remember last night."

"And this morning." She stood taller, on her toes, and gave me another kiss. Then she let me go.

Joanna came up once Chris had gone to wave off her parents. Before climbing into the Nissan, I leaned near her. "If you fuck this up for me…"

Joanna laughed harshly as she zipped up her woolen jacket. "Yes? You'll what? There's nothing you can do, Lucky. Now enjoy the drive to New Mexico. Think about what might happen. You never know, do you? I'm sorry it came to this. I liked you. I really did." She brushed her mousy blond hair behind her ear. "But I don't like people lying to my friends."

Part Two

36

I let myself in and walked down the hallway. All I remember is that I'd locked the house up that night, the night of the fight with Mike, I'd put the plants outside for people to take, and I'd driven off.

The hallway smelled stuffy and stale. The kitchen stank. I opened the fridge. Mistake. I closed the door. I sat at the square table next to the window and dropped my head onto my arms, lying there not moving. I did nothing. I sat there, head on the table, and stared off to the side. I saw a white wall, yellow counter tops, and a box of mac and cheese still unopened. I heard the kids next door, screaming and squealing as they made a snowman. I'd made it back for the snow.

It was cold in the house. In Dad's house. I stood up and walked silently back to the front door and found the thermostat. I turned it up. Had I turned if off before I left? I couldn't remember. I walked back down to the kitchen. I had nothing to drink. I opened his cupboards, looking for something, anything. I found black tea and some packets of hot chocolate. I took a packet and laid it on the table next to the range. I poured water into an old pan and put it on to boil. I watched it boil. I sat down with my mug of hot chocolate.

Lost. Lost. What do I do now? In Dad's home? Without him? I had no idea. I drank the hot chocolate slowly. I had no rush. I couldn't go back to the hospital until the next day. At noon. Another, I glanced at my phone, sixteen hours. Nothing to do. Like Dad. He lay there. I'd sat, watching him breathe. For eight hours.

I sat at his kitchen table and I did nothing. It's amazing how little anyone really needs to do, isn't it? Especially when you don't want to eat, or talk, or watch television. Nothing to do. Nothing to say. Lucky to be alone. Right?

I wandered around the kitchen, opening and closing the cupboards, sliding out the drawers, and spotted the mail piled up where I'd left it, next to the coffee pot. The bills. I could look at the bills, and pay what was most needed. I had his debit card. I'd go to the bank and pull out some cash. Where was his checkbook? I knew my pitiful savings wouldn't last much longer.

I found his wallet and stuff in the drawer under the phone. I pulled it out and looked. I tried to write his signature. Not so good. I practiced for five or six times before it would be close enough. He'd never fight me about forging his name, but I was scared that the bank knew, knew he was in hospital. I didn't want any legal hassles. Not now.

I opened some letters, and read the statements. I wanted to throw up. I hated reading his private mail. I had no choice. The mortgage had been paid off last year, so we didn't, or rather *I,* didn't need to worry about that. The electric and the gas were overdue. I wrote out two checks. The phone company threatened to cut off the cell phone. Let them. He didn't need it any more. The landline, though, was a different matter.

I walked back outside to the mailbox with the bills ready to go out, and discovered it was stuffed with junk mail, free newspapers and not much else. Nothing from his friends. Did anyone even know what had happened to him? I'd have to find the address book. I'd have to tell them. After I talked to the neurosurgeon tomorrow. Yeah, once I had some answers. If I had some answers.

Inside the house, I finally pulled out a big black bag and opened the fridge again. I didn't even check, simply dumped everything into the trash. Condiments of all kinds, the old moldy burgers, leftover pizza (mine?), solid skim milk, and two wrappers of cheese. All of it went outside into the big green can. I opened the kitchen window wide and kept both the front and back doors open even with heat pumping. Who cared?

I drank some more hot chocolate and craved a shot of something stronger. I left the kitchen and all of its dirty counters, the sink of matching blue dishes, and I went in search of my dad's booze.

The house was small, a two bedroom, one bath, on Lena, just off Second Street. A couple of blocks from the brewery. I didn't want to go there, not yet, not ready to chat to people who knew us. I needed to get out, but not like that. I knew better.

I stood on the steps briefly for a smoke. The front yard was probably ten by ten and full of weeds and shrubs. A large elm stood in the middle, dropping its leaves for my dad to rake up every October. Neither of us had done any gardening here in ages. I'd been away a month. He'd been in hospital six weeks now. The snow covered the signs of neglect. It even looked pretty. Innocent somehow.

I nodded at the ten-year-old twins, bundled up in layers, who were putting the finishing touches on their snow-dog next door. A huge pit-bull of a snow creature. I laughed and they grinned in delight. I put out the butt and closed myself back inside. I locked the door.

Silence. Profound, deep, disturbing silence greeted me, held me and wouldn't let me go. I had no words in my head. And no camera to capture how it felt to be back. To return. To a dead house. No life. No presence. I half expected Dad to come in the back, shaking off the snow and asking me how work went, before telling me about how the hike up Atalaya Trail had gone, as he pulled open the fridge for a Budweiser.

But he didn't come home.

In the living room, I made a fire. I sat in front of it and stared at the flames. I should have called Christine but I had no words. I looked around. The room was a light blue, with green chairs and a worn out sofa. The one where Dad would read at night, using the standing light behind him, and stretching his legs toward the fireplace. I moved over and sat down. I picked up the last book he'd read.

I didn't know it, but it was old school detective stories from England. *The Remorseful Day,* one of the Inspector Morse series by Colin Dexter, a reminder of his days near Oxford, maybe? He'd turned the corner of a page near the end and had put it down on the carpet before he went outside. I wonder what had taken him out late at night? What had been his last thought?

I curled up and stuck my head in the corner of the chair, smelling his aftershave and soap, noticing a stray hair lingering still.

I woke to find myself in pitch black, struggling to make sense of where I was. Home. I was home. Whatever that meant. I sat up and saw the fire had almost gone out. I made it up with some kindling and pine logs. I squatted as close as I could get. The heater was pumping, blasting out hot air and I remembered I'd left the windows open. No wonder it was freezing in here. Probably in the teens outside. Oh well. I paid the bills now, right?

I looked out the kitchen window as I ran the hot water into the sink. I stared at the snow still falling. At the cars in the driveways and the neighbors' Christmas lights, already up. The holidays. To be alone for the holidays. There's nothing like it.

37

I walked up toward the railroad tracks and turned right in the driveway. I carried a growler, the empty half-gallon glass jar that you can use for buying beer to take home. Second Street Brewery looked empty. A Monday evening. Late. Not much happening for once. At least not here. I walked up past the patio, glad that no one I knew was outside smoking. Quiet, like I said. I walked inside and up to the bar at the far end.

"Kolsch, Lucky?"

"Yeah, thanks. Nice to see you remembered," I joked. I took my leather off and kept the beanie on, half hiding under it. I sat at the stool and reached for my wallet.

"On the house. When did you get back? I heard you'd gone out to Chicago or something." Erin stood and wiped the counter top as he chatted to me about the trip, and the weather.

"Nothing on TV tonight?" I asked.

He looked up at the blank screen. "Probably, just nobody's asked so far tonight. Want to see something?"

"The Packers are playing, I think. Minnesota? Not sure. Haven't been keeping up. Have you got the remote?"

Erin reached under and found it, passing me the controls and telling me to keep the volume down. He asked about my Dad but I shrugged it off.

"I'll know more tomorrow."

"That's too bad. Well, it's good to see you back. Let me know if you need anything."

I turned on the TV and found the game. I leaned on my arms, half sleeping as I watched the plays. I thought of Christine at her kitchen table, with the books scattered and the radio playing the blues on WORT, her local public radio station that she loved so much. I drank the beer and then another. I dozed, falling into the football zone as the Packers creamed their neighbors. A good game. Even being such a wipeout for Minnesota, I admired them for trying. For keeping pressure on. Eventually, I stood outside on the back patio under the propane heaters and smoked.

"Can I join you?"

I turned to see Susan standing there, hidden in the shadows of the ash tree on the other side of the fence. I didn't know what to say. I said nothing. Where was my damn camera when I needed it? I stood and stared at her. She looked the same, as far as I could tell. A thick padded coat wrapped her up, a striped hat, and the inevitable purse across her left shoulder.

"Well? Aren't you going to invite me in?"

"It's a public place."

"Thanks," and she pushed the small wooden gate out of her way.

"Is Mike coming?" I couldn't help but ask.

She shook her head and came close, joining me next to the heaters. She shivered. We stood there in the quiet for some time before she asked me about Dad.

"I was with him today. No change, or at least as far as I'm concerned, there's no change. The nurses are upbeat, though. I don't know why."

"Yeah, I know. I've been there a few times. They let me sit with him for an hour or so. It's hard, isn't it?"

I looked down into her eyes, surprised anyone had been. Or that she would have gone. I didn't ask. I couldn't. She told me anyway.

"I went alone. Mike wanted to come with me, but I asked him not to. I needed some quiet time with your Dad. Alone, you know? There's almost a magical quality when you look at him lying there."

I laughed, soft and bitter, both. I shrugged deeper into my jacket. The snow kept falling. Later than usual, but the cold meant it'd stay for the holidays. The holidays. Ah, crap.

"Another beer?" I turned back to Susan. The one I'd lived with for five years. My girlfriend. I held out my hand to her and she took it, gratefully. We stood for a moment and then both reached for the door handle at the same time.

We sat at the bar for another two hours. The game forgotten. Susan told me of the radio station's newest employee, a charmer of an Australian, all talk, but in a way that the managers and listeners alike fell for. But not me, she laughed. No more relationships for me!

"What about Mike? Doesn't he count?" I asked.

She had the decency to blush. She took her hat off and rubbed a hand through her hair. It looked different somehow. Maybe it was my memory gone bad? It wouldn't surprise me at this point. Remembering a hairstyle was not a high priority for me. "He and I. Well, it was a mistake. Sex, attention, you know how it is. A bad decision. I'm so sorry, Lucky." She turned to me, her eyes telling me the honesty of that, what—disclaimer? Excuse? I asked for a bottle of water from Erin and the tab. He passed up the growler. I left a hefty tip.

"I have to go home."

"You staying at your Dad's?"

I nodded and grabbed my jacket and the beer. I leaned in and gave her a quick kiss on the cheek and walked out.

38

"Lucky Phillips?"

I looked up, reluctantly lifting my head from the bed. I'd fallen asleep with my head on Dad's bed. His hand in mine. The repetitive beeping and the rattle in his chest put me to sleep.

I saw an older woman in her fifties holding out her hand to me. She wore her lab coat wrapped around black pants and a plain dark brown jacket. Her hair was tied back in a ponytail, with her glasses up on her forehead, out of the way.

"I'm Dr. Kate Smith. The neurosurgeon. Do you have a moment?"

We both looked at my Dad and I tried not to laugh at the absurd question. I stood up, with my knees shaking, and my hands sweating. I needed a glass of water. Another hangover lingering past mid-day. Not a good sign.

Dr. Smith led me out the security doors, and we both washed our hands under the faucets. A religion here in ICU, washing hands, disinfecting, cleaning, wiping. I'd been sent home that first day, told to come back in clean jeans and shirt. To have a shower next time I wanted to come in there. Embarrassed, I'd come back two hours later with clothes straight from Wal-Mart. I'd washed at the house, reluctantly using Dad's towels and soap.

We stepped past the other families waiting, heads resting in hands, sitting on the plastic seats, magazines opened uselessly on their laps. I knew. They knew. We avoided eye contact. Too much pain. Just another day at the V.A.

We walked down past another set of doors and into the 'family' room on the left. In here they had a small fridge for tea, coffee and cream. A TV was up in the high far corner, turned off. The room was tiny, and filled with comfortable armchairs and a sofa. Dr. Smith sat opposite me. "Something to drink?"

"Water, please."

A few moments later, I could avoid it no more. I looked up. She was watching me, waiting for me.

"Now, to start with, before I answer your questions, I need you to tell me what you know."

I shrugged. No words.

"I need you to talk to me, Lucky. I know how hard this can be, but I need to know what you've heard from the nurses, the other doctors, your girlfriend."

"Ex. Ex-girlfriend." I looked up to add quickly, "But it's okay for her to come here still, isn't it? He needs visitors, you know?" My eyes teared up slightly and I reached for the glass of cold water. Tasted good to me. I started to tell her about the research I'd done, reading about this stuff. How I'd been away, and didn't really see any difference in him since the end of October. "They told me he's doing well. That his heart rate is better and his lungs cleared up after that scare. One nurse said he responds to her, when she talks to him. She said it looks good. He's getting better."

There was a silence. The doctor didn't move or say anything. I looked up. She shook her head ever so slightly.

"What? What?" I could barely hear myself, I spoke so quietly.

Dr. Smith sat forward in her chair. She sighed and put her notes on her lap, reaching for a glass of water, herself. "It's the nurses' job to stay positive. How else could they do what they do? I don't know. I come in and out every week and so I see the bigger picture. I'll keep this as simple as possible. Lucky, we really don't expect your Dad to come back. Not like he was. Right now, we're still watching and waiting. He did respond to some tests last week and so that gave us hope, but we did another MRI and that came back today. It's not good." She drank a whole glassful and filled us both back up. "Do you have any other family?"

I shook my head slowly.

"Your girlfriend, sorry, ex-girlfriend seems to really care about him. And I'm glad. For you both, I'd say."

"Why does that matter?"

"This is a long term, not a quick fix situation. If we're going to aim for an ongoing slow recovery, you need to take care of yourself. Eat healthy foods, sleep, work, and take care of the rest of your life." She looked at her notes briefly. "You have asked about what to expect, is that right?"

I nodded uncertainly.

"Like I said, we have to mix positive hope and reality, both. My job is to assess your Dad's brain. The level of damage and the potential for recovery."

"Most strokes get better, though, don't they? I read about the rehab and how slow it is, and I'm fine with that. I can help Dad. I have nothing else to do. I can help."

"By taking care of yourself. Ask your friends to help you."

"Help me do what?"

"Get back on track. I don't like to betray a confidence, but Susan mentioned the break up and losing your dog and then your job. She said you just disappeared for weeks. She's also a bit worried about your drinking."

I hung my head. I didn't want to lie. I had nothing to say, though.

"This is what I mean, Lucky. Ask your friends. Talk to them. Or a counselor, perhaps? Someone you trust."

At that, I laughed. "If only it was so easy," I muttered.

Dr. Smith let me gather myself a moment before continuing with her news. "There has been severe damage to your dad's brain. The areas most affected are not going to come back. The problem is that I don't see any other pathways for those messages to be sent; it's like there's been a rockslide on the main highway and we're waiting to see if a detour will be found."

"Is there nothing you can do? Surgery?"

She shook her head. "I'm sorry. But no, in your Dad's case, there is very little anyone can do. We'll take another scan this weekend and I'll meet you on Tuesday to talk about the results. In the meantime, Henry is stable, he's breathing without any more pneumonia clogging his lungs, and he's not rejecting the pain meds. We'll go with that as good news. However, you do need to think about his quality of life. And yours. As the sole family member, you need to be aware of how much this will affect you, taking care of him for a long time."

"Weeks?"

"Years."

I sat back and closed my eyes. Oh, Dad. What has become of us?

"Lucky?"

I looked over to her.

"Does Henry have any other family? Relatives?"

"He goes by Bill, not Henry. And yes, he has a daughter. My half-sister. I've never met her, though. Why?"

Dr. Smith just left me to think about it before asking, "Does Bill have a will that you know of? Or a living will? Someone with the Medical Power of Attorney?"

"You're the second person to ask me that. I have no idea. Why?"

"If he does, we need to respect his wishes."

I shook my head, uncomprehending.

"If he doesn't come out of this vegetative state by Christmas, he never will. We need to face the fact that your Dad might not want to live like this. If he had a choice."

I hung my head, staring at my hands as they dangled uselessly across my knees. My boots needed a good clean. I looked up. "I'll look into it. Next week? We'll know more?"

Dr. Smith stood and closed her jacket up, held out her hand to me again, and promised we'd talk more then. I watched the long brown ponytail get caught in her collar as she leaned down to get her files. I reached to untuck her hair, but stopped myself just in time. "Lucky? Remember to take care of yourself. That's all you can really do for him now. Live your own life." She shut the door quietly behind her. I listened to the footsteps heading back to the ICU, the pause at the sink, and the sound of the automatic doors opening and closing.

"Fuck!" I kicked the table across the room. All five feet of it. It didn't help. I sat and stared out the hospital window for an hour before walking back the way we'd come. I found my Dad, and took his hand in mine. I stroked the soft skin, and turned his hand over, looking for the scar I'd put there one time as a seven-year-old with a temper. I touched it to my lips.

"I'm sorry, Dad."

39

I answered the knock in my Dad's robe. I'd been wandering around the kitchen and well, the whole house, thinking is this what's left? His stuff? My memories? Is this it? What it comes to?

I wasn't expecting anyone. No one knew I'd come back. As far as I knew. I scratched my hair into some semblance of tidiness, tucked in the belt and opened the door wide.

Mike stood there in his green army coat and a black cowboy hat, smiling as if nothing had changed. He stepped forward and past me, heading down the corridor and into the kitchen. He sniffed at the coffee in the pot.

"How long has this been sitting here?" he asked. "Since yesterday?"

"Last night. I couldn't sleep so I sat here and drank coffee, daydreaming, I guess."

Mike emptied it out in the sink and filled it with fresh water and grounds. He turned it on and then leaned back against the counter. I sat down and retied Dad's robe. I looked over at him. He smiled, a softer version than before.

"How's your Dad?"

"Why?"

"Oh, don't be an idiot. He's like an uncle to me. Family. How is he?"

"He won't be coming back."

My bleak statement was met with stunned silence. I'd had a week to get used to the idea, since the last meeting with Dr. Smith. Kate. I didn't know how to put it gently.

"I'm sorry, Mike, but that's the reality of it right now. The doctor says it's not looking good for the old man. If he was younger, maybe, but even then, there's too much damage."

The coffee pot sang its call to action. We sat with mugs, sugar and cream between us. I pulled out a smoke and lit up. Mike stared at me in surprise.

"But you can't smoke in here!"

"Why not? He's not coming back, Mike. It doesn't matter. It doesn't matter."

I rested my head on the table. He didn't move. For that, I was glad. I didn't know how to deal with him here. We drank down our coffee, two mugs full each. The heat kicked in.

I stood up, walked into my room, and picked up the clothes from the day before. I realized they stank of cigarettes and beer. I threw them aside and chose another version of the same outfit. Black jeans, a non-descript black t-shirt, gray socks. I wore colors that suited my mood those days.

Back in the kitchen, Mike hadn't moved. He looked up at me with tears in his eyes. "I'm sorry," he muttered

"For what?" I snapped.

"Well, everything. Your dad. Susan. Blue. But there's nothing I can do."

I sat down opposite him and we simply stared at each for a moment. Mike took his coat off, and tucked the dark green shirt into the finely pressed blue jeans. He scratched the beginnings of a beard.

"How did you know I was back?" I asked him eventually.

"Susan told me."

"You still speak to her?"

"Yeah." He gave a wry smile. "A flash in the pan. Nothing lasting. I'm sorry. Honestly, Lucky. Anyway, Susan and I've been good friends for years—I'm just glad I didn't fuck that part up, too." He looked at me briefly. "I know there's nothing I can do to help your Dad. But can I help you? Somehow? Anything?"

I stood up suddenly and the chair fell back and crashed. Mike flinched. I laughed bitterly. Harshly.

"No. I don't think so. I'd say you've done enough, but that's such a cliché, isn't it?"

He watched me pace the room, and when I circled behind him, he'd tense up but he never moved away. He trusted me still? After what I did to him?

"How *is* the knee, by the way?"

I stood in the back doorway, looking out the window onto the trees and the snow drifts. I turned to see him move his leg unconsciously. He grimaced, not knowing I was watching. "Is it going to be okay?" I asked.

"Yeah. It'll take time, the doctor said. But it's a good reminder. Don't worry about it, Lucky. It's done."

I sat back down, my anger gone as quickly as a flash flood. The damage was done, as he said. I sighed. I rested my head on the tabletop again.

"Want to go for a beer, Lucky?"

I looked up and checked the clock. Eleven o'clock already? How could that be? "It's time for me to drive to Albuquerque, see Dad at the hospital. I should have a shower, get ready, you know? I need to be there."

"You also need to take time for yourself. That's what Susan told me. The doctors told you that, too, didn't they?"

I nodded but stood to get ready regardless.

"No, wait, Lucky. Come out with me. It'll be good for you. We don't have to talk about any of this stuff. Just go to the Cowgirl, or Second Street or somewhere completely different downtown. Or into the hills. I bet you haven't been up to the Sangres yet, have you? It'll be good to get out, honest! Take a day off. Or an afternoon off, at least. Susan said she was going visit him after work. It's Thursday, she's done by two. She could be there by three or so."

I couldn't decide. But I knew he was right. They were right. Sitting by the hospital bed, holding Dad's hand, not talking or moving, just watching him, I couldn't do it for much longer. Something had to change. Mike saw me trying to decide and offered to call Susan to check, to ask her to go visit Dad since he was taking me out of the house. I nodded.

"Okay. Give me a minute."

We parked his Chevy up at the trailhead. I stretched up tall and looked around. Snow everywhere, thick and untouched by human or dog alike. Aspens bent under the weight of the snow, frozen in place. I breathed in deeply. I listened to the silence. I tucked in my hair, under the beanie, and found the gloves in my pocket. Mike did the same.

We didn't speak, just nodded when we were both ready and then we set out. A steady climb through the thick snow base kept me focused on breathing. I had no words. And no camera. I hadn't told him anything yet. I didn't want to just forgive and forget. I couldn't. We hiked up two miles to the corner peak, where the vista opens up to the whole Santa Fe valley, glistening in the sunlight. A few stray clouds hovered over the Sandia Mountains, we saw a bird or two, ravens, probably, but that was it. I stood and took a huge deep breath and let it out with a scream.

Mike laughed and then did the same and suddenly we were both yelling and swearing and screaming and shouting and throwing snowballs at each other and running and flinging and laughing until we fell into a heap by the creek bed. Exhausted but happy. The question was who collapsed first. And why.

"I blame the altitude! I can't breathe."

"I blame the knee! I can't run."

We both lay there, panting and staring up through the bare aspen branches to the blue sky above.

Mike sat up and wiped himself down. "Do you ever think of Blue?"

"I try not to."

"I do. I miss her. I read in the paper the other day how this woman lost her dog in La Cienega and she was frantic. She made fliers and posted them all over the state, as far as Questa and Ruidoso! She never gave up, checking in with the shelters and in the papers."

"And the moral of the story is?" I asked sarcastically.

"She found her lab in Las Vegas two months later. Someone had taken him in, but it didn't work out." He paused. "I know it's not something you have time, or energy for, but can I look for her again? I did when you first left town. I called the shelter, put an ad in the Reporter, Craigslist, that kind of thing. But I stopped. I want to try again. Is that okay?"

"Yeah. Good luck." I stood and he followed suit. We headed back down to the truck; both of us were quiet, each lost in our heads, I guess. I stopped him as he took his coat off and opened the driver's door.

"Thanks, Mike."

He nodded and climbed inside. He leaned over to open my door, asking, "Beer?"

"Sounds good to me."

40

I had to go through Dad's stuff. The doctors made it clear that someone needed to take care of business. Whatever that meant. I had no idea.

I started in the kitchen, slowly going through each and every drawer. In one, I found packs of old photographs, of us when I was a kid, a few of us moving here to New Mexico when I was a teenager, before he sent me off. I opened an old brown envelope and saw Mom.

She sat cross-legged on a blanket under an apricot tree. The tree was raining flowers on her and her face was turned up, as she laughed. The black and white photo was not one I'd seen before. To be honest, Dad had kind of hidden the photos of Mom after the funeral. One framed photo of them on their wedding day, and another of me as an infant on her lap. Those were the only two I grew up with.

I sat down and held the photos to my chest. I quickly started opening every drawer in the house, riffling through whatever I found, looking for Mom and Dad. There was a knock at the door but I ignored it. I kept searching. Searching for signs of life.

The living room looked as if a drag queen had thrown a hissy fit. I sat in the middle with the albums on my knees, and the fire going to my right. I had a light turned low. I slowly went through each album, page by page. I kept turning backwards and forwards, grasping at memories, feeding myself with stories.

"Do you remember that time at the waterfall in Colorado, Dad? When we'd gone camping and found this path along the mountain's edge? I remember being thrilled that we'd found our own secret garden and I ran ahead. You heard my yell and came running to catch me, save me, I don't know what. You found me staring wide-eyed and in shock at the height of this waterfall. You came up and shouted over the din it made, *Want to go underneath it?* I didn't know what you meant so you told me to get undressed and to follow you. I did. And, naked, we ran under the river crashing down hundreds of feet. You held my hand and we squealed together at how cold it was. But then you laughed and pointed to the path we'd come along. There stood a bus load of gray-haired tourists, slack-jawed in the shock of seeing us in all our glory!"

I stroked his hand and looked up. His eyes flickered over toward me and I stood up so quickly the seat dropped back down with a crash. I yelled, "Nurse! He heard me, he heard me! Look!" I talked to Dad again and his eyes stayed facing me, unfocused and lost, but there, they were there, looking at me. "He hasn't done that before, it's good, right? That he can hear me?" I was panting in shock, excitement. Dad. He could hear me. The nurse read the machines above his head and patted me on the arm.

"No, Lucky, it doesn't mean he can hear you, not like you want him to. Something in there responded to sound, or emotion. I don't know. But he's not there, not as your dad used to be."

She sat me down again and told me to keep talking to him anyway.

"Hearing is the last thing that goes. So it's worth telling him stories, my dear. Tell him everything. Everything you need to say. This is the time."

I looked at him and back to her. She shook her head sadly and walked back to her station opposite his bed. I leaned in and stared into his eyes. They rolled around but he didn't see me. I broke down.

41

"The house is a wreck," Susan politely pointed out as she let herself in. I hadn't answered the front door.

Calling out to me as she came down the hallway, she'd found me in the living room, with papers and files and books and photographs scattered around me. The place was dark but for one candle on the tabletop. I sat in Dad's pajamas, with tears pouring down my face. I looked away but she saw.

"Oh, Lucky." She fell to her knees and grabbed me to her, holding and rocking me against her. She stroked my head, wiping away the tears as they continued to fall.

"I can't do this. I can't do this," I whispered. I kept saying it over and over, loudly, softly, raging and then in fear. Susan rocked me until I let it all go. She held me. Finally, I was spent. I didn't move. I sat back and tucked in my pajamas, and let out a huge sigh. Sorry, I apologized. She laughed gently.

"Right. Like you need to!" She stood up. "Tea? Coffee?"

"Tea, please, that'd be nice. Thanks."

"Sure."

I watched her take off her coat and lay it across the armchair, putting the purse next to it. She glanced at the drawers empty and thrown on the table, the empty mugs leaving marks on the wood, and candle wax dripping from beer bottles. She shook her head slightly and went to put the teakettle on. I lay back and stared at the fireplace.

"This isn't like you, Lucky" she said when she came back. "To live in a mess like this. What's going on?"

I took the tea from her and made room on the floor next to me. She knelt down and stretched out her legs, leaning back against the sofa.

"Dad's not coming back."

"I know that but why let this all go to the dumps? You have to live here. You *are* going to keep living here, right?"

"I don't know. I don't know what I'm doing. But the counselor at the hospital tells me I have to take care of business. I started to look for his papers, you know?" I sipped the tea gratefully. Beer was no longer helping me. "And then I found all these photos yesterday and then I had to find the rest. This is it." I pointed to a box, well, a suitcase-sized pile of photos. We both stared at them in their chaos.

"That's wonderful, Lucky. Look at them all!"

"It is and it isn't. What am I supposed to do with all his stuff? Do I keep everything? Do I throw it all out? What do I do? Look, the place is packed with Dad's stuff and I don't know what to do!" I poked at the fire.

"It's fine, and you don't need to do that." Susan took the stick out of my hands. "What do you need to find? What do really need to take care of?"

"A will. She said I have to see if he has a will, or had any legal papers. Power of Attorney, that kind of thing. And I have a sister somewhere. I don't know her name, nothing. I should tell her. His friends. I have to call them, but I can't do it." I put the mug down. I wanted a cigarette but they weren't helping, either.

Susan took out a notepad from her purse and started to write. "Banks. Will. Family? Do you know when she was born? Or where? I might be able to research her through some contacts at work. They know how to look up and verify stuff like this."

I stretched my legs out and laid my head across her lap. I told her what I knew about this sister of mine. Arizona. A June baby. Sometime when I was six or seven.

"So that makes her thirty-ish, right?"

"Yep. This'll be a shock. I don't know if they stayed in touch."

"Why didn't your dad talk about her?"

"I stabbed him with a knife when I was a kid. I didn't like the idea of sharing him!"

She laughed. "Temper! Temper!"

I poked her knee and then grabbed her foot, tickling her. She slapped me across the head and told me to cut it out, but she laughed and didn't throw me off. I lay back against her and talked of Dad and Mom, when we lived in Oxford. I talked of the low green hills covered with trees and woods, just perfect for kids to chase around in, the canals, the meadows and farmland between every village where they let me fly my kites. The cows came up to me, a curious kid, and I stroked them and pulled on their ears and they never blinked. I talked of the potato fields I rode my bike across, flying over the bumps and ridges, grabbing a few for dinner. I talked of the winding narrow roads that linked town to town, and the constant rain that drove my mom silly and how I didn't care whether it rained or not, I'd be outside playing with Mike on the swings or in the fields by the base. I talked and talked. Susan listened.

"Okay, lets get down to work." She stood up, turned on the overhead lights, and stretched her arms, arching backwards and showing a stripe of belly skin. A place I knew so well. I reached for her but dropped my hands to my sides before she noticed. Her light yellow t-shirt reflected in the bright white lights. The blue jeans hugged her body nicely, but that's no surprise, she'd always taken good care of herself. I noticed my own ragged appearance in the window. The pajamas I'd worn all week. The hair grown out in all directions. The fingernails, broken and dirty. A mess. I was a mess.

"I'll have a bath first, if that's okay. I'd like to clean up a bit. Starting with me, I guess." She assessed me and grinned, "Good idea. I'll clean up in here, make some order of your chaos. Don't worry, I won't throw anything away, I'll just organize stuff. Take your time, Lucky. There's no rush."

The clock told me it was ten at night.

"But don't you have to get home?" I asked.

"Go have a bath. Come back out when you're ready to work," and she pushed me in the right direction.

In the kitchen, Susan was piling up the bank statements, the house bills, and personal letters—all the things she found in, under, and on top of the surfaces. She'd cleaned out one of the cupboards, too, making another stack on the floor in a brown paper bag. The radio was tuned to KBAC, of course, her station, and an Australian voice chatted away, making Susan laugh to herself. I stood a moment, taking it all in before I stepped in, ready for the next phase.

"Hey." I sat down and reached for a bottle of water. "How can I help?"

"Take out that bag of food, to start with. We can make some space. Mostly I want to get you comfortable in here, and hopefully we can set you up to pay the monthly bills on time. We'll see if we find any mention of your sister in the paperwork. Did you remember her name?"

I looked inside the bags to find cans of tuna, black beans and packets of soup. Outdated by months and in some cases, years. "Helen."

"Really? That's great. Good job, that'll help."

"Unless she kept Dad's name. Helen Phillips won't exactly stand out in the crowd, will it?"

Susan shrugged and issued her orders. "Don't worry about that. It's time to work. Starting now, take it all out back, will you?"

I put on the coat and stood outside for a moment, enjoying half a cigarette in the moonlight. A half moon was waxing and the clouds stayed away. Inside, I saw Susan add something to one of the piles, picking at her nails as she concentrated on a letter. Her phone rang and she picked it up, taking it with her down the hallway, to talk privately.

I let myself back in and rested against the counter, then picked up the pile closest. His letters.

42

"What shall we do with these?"

Susan came over to me and picked up a couple of his letters and looked at the names.

"I guess we need to call them. Let them know what's going on. Do you know any of them?"

"A couple sound familiar, but no, not anyone I met. At least, not so far. I found his address book. Could you? Work your way through it sometime? I can't. I can't do it."

Susan took the book saying she'd call in the morning. We took another hour going through what we could find in the kitchen and living room. Neither of us wanted to go into his bedroom. She asked me about my plans. I didn't have any.

The radio played some Coldplay and Phish. That time of night, I guess. We sat in the kitchen and sorted out the details, who she'd contact, and we made a list for me. As next of kin, it was up to me to talk to the banks and various companies. I put her notes next to the phone.

We sat there. Outside, the night held secrets and the streets kept quiet.

"We need to talk." She spoke up suddenly.

I laughed. Not what I'd wanted to hear. I shook my head. "No, please no. I can't take on any more. I don't have anything to say to you, Susan."

"But I do."

We sat at the wooden kitchen table, a pot of tea between us, and the heater hummed in the background. She put on her wool sweater, and reached for her own pile of notes and envelopes.

"Let's just talk," she said with a smile. I nodded but waited. What did she need to tell me? I pulled out the tobacco, and rolled a smoke. I waited. She brushed her hair into place, checked her nails and then her phone. I waited. She finally looked over to me.

"I've met someone."

"Oh, really?"

She didn't say anything for a while. We listened to the radio announcer joking about the commercial for Budweiser tasting like piss-water. Susan laughed to herself. I grinned.

"Him?"

She looked up at me, surprised. "Yeah. How'd you know?"

I had to laugh. "I know you," I told her, "and I know how you laugh when you like someone!" She had the honesty to admit that yes, it was David, the Australian at work. We chatted about him and how they met, how it became more than a casual fling. She'd wanted to tell me over the last couple of weeks, but hadn't known how. And then I told her about Christine, and how easy it was with her. A best friend and lover, both.

"Like we'd been?" she teased.

I gave her a nod and told her how Chris and I talk and laugh and play, and how it became more sexual just before I left. In a whole new way. Then I told her about Michaela and my obsession, my need to see her, to be alone with her. The shame of my desire for her. The games we'd played. The roles I'd played for her. Of what she'd done.

"But why shame?"

I described how uncomfortable and out of control I was when I was with her. I'd send messages and wait and check to see if she'd get back in touch, and how I'd find her with her friends, take photos of them together, only to pour over the images later that night when Chris was studying.

"Good Girl versus Bad Girl?"

I laughed at that. "Perfect! Yeah, that's it! And each one so easily embodies the good and the bad instinctively. Although Michaela has been nothing but honest with me." I stood and walked to the nicely cleaned fridge and opened it to pull out a beer. "Want one?" Susan nodded. I brought them both over as she smiled.

I used the leprechaun novelty opener we'd brought back from Ireland. A present for Dad. With a sad smile, we toasted each other. A clink and then we both took a sip, put the Pale Ales down, and carried on. The radio interrupted us with some announcement or other and I caught her eye, toasted her, and sat back in the chair. I talked more about my time in Madison.

"Michaela told me from day one that she liked affairs, flings, nothing deeper than that. She liked her time to herself, working a few hours each day, and then writing or painting or playing with her lovers but only when she wanted to. Nothing more than that was ever offered. I don't know why I went along with it. You know me, that's not my style."

Susan sipped her beer. "Not that I'd noticed! But it makes sense, you had a rough time and needed something different, right?"

"Yeah, I guess."

"And now? Have you called either of them?"

We both looked at the phone on the wall, silent and untouched, and we laughed out loud.

"No. I didn't know what to say." A helpless knowing shrug of my shoulders.

"You never do!" She raised her drink at me in toast. "Friends?"

"Yeah, friends." I looked down sheepishly, not quite sure what to do or say. The clock ticked away. We ended up chatting more about her new beau and mine. The two of them, Good Girl and Bad. What to do? Who to call?

43

I woke up to furious knocking at the front door. I struggled into the robe and stumbled to the front door. It was just barely light out.

"What the fuck?" I yelled as I opened the door.

Mike stood there, practically jumping up and down. He pushed me back in, holding his phone out to me. "Listen to this, Lucky!"

"No! What? What are you doing here, Mike? It's not even seven!"

Mike strode back into the kitchen, dumping his phone in my hand and I heard him setting the coffee pot into action. I followed him in and stood against the sink. I scratched my head and tucked in the robe, wishing the heat would kick in. I got up and walked to the thermostat and boosted it a good shot.

Mike poured us both a decent mug of coffee and passed me the sugar and an ashtray. He sat down. He could barely contain himself. His feet tapped rhythmically on the Saltillo tiles. I waited. I looked at the pile Susan had left next to the phone. People to call. Notes to follow up on. I looked back to Mike. He leaned back in the chair, and then looked up at me. "I've found Blue!" he told me. "I mean, I *think* I've found Blue!"

I put the mug down. I stared at him. Was this some joke? Some kind of payback?

Mike leaned forward. "I called all the shelters in the state. Each and every one. Oh, my God, there's a lot! Anyway, I left messages. I described her, a sweet but shy collie and lab mix, red collar, her name, all of it."

I drank my coffee and I smoked. I waited. I sat down.

"Jackie from Taos called me back yesterday. She told me how they had a female dog that fitted my description. She'd been with them for the last month, more or less. It's the end of her time there. She'll be put down this week! We have to go. Now. We have to go and see if it's her! Now, Lucky. Today!" Mike stood up and took my mug from me. I had all these questions but he wouldn't let me talk. "Now. Get dressed. I'll tell you what I know on the drive up there, okay? I promise. We'll be back in time for you to get to the hospital this afternoon. Come on! It really could be Blue!"

We stopped at Aztec Street café for a huge mug of coffee each to go. That and breakfast burritos with bacon and green chile. Mike drove, trying to keep to the speed limits on the way through Pojoaque and into Espanola. Shania Twain came on the radio—92.3 is not my favorite station, but it worked that day. I curled up deeper into my leather jacket and hid behind my sunglasses. The mountains shimmered with new snowfall. The heat blasted away and I opened the window, smoking and enjoying the crisp air, both. Mike talked nine to the dozen.

"Jackie told me how this girl dog came in; she'd been picked up by some hippies in a school bus. They'd found her in the Sangre de Christos around Halloween. She'd been skinny and desperately friendly, jumping into the bus at the trailhead. She'd lost her collar but there was something domesticated about her, the way she listened. The couple fed her, and took her with them, up into the mountains around Penasco, Red River, all the national forest campsites. But then something happened. I'm not sure what. But whatever it was, they took her to the shelter and dropped her off with a bag of dog food. No numbers or names given. That was over a month ago."

I finally spoke. "And they kept her all this time? In the kennel?"

He nodded and sipped his coffee, putting it between his legs as he sped up into the gorge. The sun shone down on me and I wished I had a baseball hat with me.

"They kept her because she was so sensitive. A sweet girl. But they need to make room. Jackie, the one at the front desk, told me that it was amazing timing as the dog is scheduled to be euthanized on Friday. We have to see if it's her, right?"

"What if it's not?" I had to ask. Not used to good news.

Mike shrugged and drove faster through the curves and past a few tourists out sightseeing. "We'll find out in another hour."

He drove us deeper into the canyon and I saw the empty riverbed, waiting for the spring snowmelt to bring out the white water rafting and kayaks. The cabins in the hills all had smoke in the chimneys and the fields were golden brown. Hardly any traffic on the roads meant that Mike pushed it. We said little else. I finished the coffee. I smoked some more.

"We're here to meet Jackie." Mike took over.

I stood behind him, hidden in my winter coat. I stared around the shelter. The smell of disinfectant and dogs made me sick. I waited. Speechless. Mike and Jackie talked; he walked off with her to chat quietly. I said nothing. I couldn't. The yellow walls were covered in photographs of people of all ages and the animals they'd adopted. A wall of fame. The success stories. I studied the faces in each one. The animals' expressions. The human delight. With the same background in each one.

I looked back around me. This room. This was the room. For meeting, for paperwork, and where you'd leave with your new best friend. I almost threw up.

Jackie and Mike came back over to me. He shrugged. He didn't know yet. We followed her down the hallway and into the dog section. The adoptable dogs. I followed behind Mike. The walls closed in on me.

I remembered Blue as a puppy, following me everywhere, coming to the studio, sleeping at my feet when I took the orders for prints, when I found the right kind of film and lenses. How Blue would fall asleep on my jacket, and then wake up needing to pee. I had to watch her closely and throw her out as soon as I saw her start to stir. Many a mess! The owner and photographer, Jonathon, had loved her, though, so it wasn't a big deal, thankfully. I remembered how she'd slept with her head on my heart after Dad had his stroke. She'd slept there all night, as I lay there, stunned, silent and immobile. My gentle friend of the last six years. Blue. Blue.

Jackie opened a door and ushered us through. It was a small white and green concrete room with a bed in the far corner, a bowl of water next to it and a doggy door to a small yard outback. I heard Mike cry out. And Blue barked, and barked and hid back in the corner barking at us both. I fell to my knees and called to her, sweet nothings only she knew. I held out my hand to her, tears streaming down my face, sick to my stomach, unable to move, unable to reach her. I talked and talked and called her by all the nicknames I'd ever had for her.

Mike stood behind me, and I heard him talk to Jackie. They both backed out and the door closed. I sat and stretched out my hands. I talked softly, on and on. I said everything, I told her about Dad. I told her about Susan and Mike. Christine and Michaela. Frank. Daniel. The photography show. All of it.

The door opened and Mike came in to find me on the cold concrete floor with Blue on my lap, my eyes still streaming, my voice still talking and talking to her. I told her everything. Mike crouched down next to us. He held out his hand to Blue and she wagged her tail but stayed with me. She was skinnier than I knew, but her eyes shone and her tail wagged. Mike laughed when she suddenly licked his face. He smiled at me, and asked, "Shall we go, Lucky? Ready to go home, Blue?"

Blue sat with me, looked into my eyes and when I nodded, she stood up and waited for me, her tail half-mast, uncertain, a slow scared wagging. I held out my hand. She sniffed it and waited at the door for us both.

"Come on, girl. Let's go home."

44

That week before Christmas, I spent my mornings at the dog park with Blue, walking the paths through the sandy arroyos, watching her play with a few other dogs, but she was so nervous, mostly she focused on the truck and on me. Not trusting me to stay with her. She came to the hospital with me, sitting with her head on my lap the whole commute to the VA hospital in Albuquerque, and once there, she waited in the truck and kept my seat warm. She gave me an excuse to leave the bed once every couple of hours and breathe in the winter cold air outside.

With being spoiled by all of us, Blue quickly gained back some weight. She was becoming fat and happy again. Well, getting there. She lay on the couch at home, at Dad's house, and she got used to Mike and Susan coming and going in the evenings. The three of us cooked together, reading different letters to each other, and remembering stories Dad had told us.

Susan called his friends from the house, and I'm glad I was there because every so often I took the phone from her to talk, to tell what I knew. Blue lay at my feet and watched me. My moods. She lay her head on my lap whenever the tears came. She sat by the door in the mornings when it was time for the drive to the hospital. I took the smell of her to Dad. The story of her to Dad. I held his hand and told him about my days.

Every day they asked if I'd found any more legal papers. I shook my head and turned back to my Dad. He never did focus on me again. Just that once. But I hoped. I hoped to get through to him, though.

I walked up the driveway with Blue at my side. She suddenly ran ahead of me, barking at some figure on the front steps. I slowed down.

"Did you forget your keys, Mike?" I called out, laughing.

Blue barked and wagged her tail and ran closer. Christine stood up.

"Are you always this late home?" she asked with a nervous smile. Blue ran around her, barking; *I like this person! I like this person! Who is she?*

"Is this Blue?" Chris held out her hand. Blue came close but watched warily until I crouched down and introduced her to Christine. "Yeah, she had quite an adventure, poor girl. Blue, this is Chris. She's come to stay with us." I stood up and came closer, shy suddenly. I stood there awkwardly.

"Aren't you going to invite me in to warm up?" she asked eventually.

"Oh, right. Sorry. How long have you been here, Chris?" I fumbled with the key and showed her the way to the kitchen, glad it was no longer a disaster area. I took her coat from her and sat her in Dad's chair, facing the window. She talked about the flights and the train and the bus and—

"The waiting. I'm sorry! I go to the hospital from noon to eight every day, more or less. Takes an hour to get back. Well. It's a long day. Want some tea?"

"Hot chocolate?"

I laughed. "Of course! Coming right up." And I looked over to her, her eyes told of fear, and of uncertainty. I knelt in front of her, stroking her face and tucking the stray hairs behind her ears, then I pulled her toward me and I hugged her.

"I'm glad you're here." We stayed like that for a while, until she reminded me she needed hot chocolate. I grinned as I got up and opened the cupboards. "It's here somewhere. And a fire? Shall we make a fire in the living room? Like we did at your house?"

Christine helped make the chocolate the old fashioned way on the stovetop, stirring the milk and cocoa powder, and leaning against me as we chatted about Blue arriving in Taos.

Chris had gained some weight, had a softness to her face, a winter layer to cuddle. I held her as we talked and I even laughed once or twice. I poured out two mugs. She followed me down the hall and into the front room. Piles of photographs lay on the table. Candles were half-burnt in bottles. Incense had obviously been used in abundance, partly from the smells sticking around, and the ash on the fireplace mantle. Home. It felt like a home, warm and welcoming. I'd had no idea.

We found the old newspapers and made a fire together, hardly moving more than a few feet away from each other at any time.

"Oh shit, my bags! I left them on the porch!" and she jumped up to get them. "I have something for you."

I heard the door open and close, then her steps came back slower than before. She brought in an old school '70s brown suitcase and placed it down near us. The fire kicked in, huge flames and dramatic flickerings. I drank the last of the chocolate and poked the fire anyway. I looked at Christine.

She sat next to the suitcase in her blue jeans and green sweatshirt. She took off her winter boots and messed with the stripy socks for a moment. She played with her hair, glanced at me, and then opened the case. She pulled out something and closed it up. She gave me my camera.

I froze.

Crap.

I stared at the camera. I wanted to take it, but I froze. I looked at Christine, who was watching me. Neither of us spoke. I understood.

"You know?"

"What's on there?" she asked.

I nodded, still unable to move.

"Yes, I know. Joanna gave it to me last week. She said she'd had it since the night before you left. I'd asked her if there was anything new on there, and her reply was really vague; 'Nothing you haven't seen before,' and she left me holding your camera. I found a box to send it on to you. I figured this was a time in your life you'd need to record."

I nodded again, scared to say more. Chris leaned back against the sofa and stared into the fire. She took a moment, adjusting her jeans and tucking the t-shirt in, before going on. "I packed it all up, wrote a letter for you and was going to send it the next day. But then I had a rough night's sleep, so I came and got it from the table. I took it out, turned it on and looked. I saw the, what it was I don't know, but the pain in your eyes, when you were undressing, stripping for Michaela. Those last photos. And I cried for you."

She turned to me, her eyes wet and overflowing. I made to reach for her, but she shook her head, no. I waited.

"I looked at each and every photo you'd taken since losing Susan. The drive out to Madison, the candid ones of me, the naked ones of the both of us, Michaela and me. And suddenly I understood so much more than I had when you were with me. The extent of the chaos in your head. That's not a judgment, by the way! No, it's just, I liked you, and I didn't see more than that, my crush and my need to study." She poked at the fire, and then with a grin she passed the poker back to me. "I study to escape, you know that, right? I can't risk getting stuck in my parents' life. It's not for me."

"Yeah, *that* I do understand."

"Well, anyway, I had these photos of you and another woman, and I saw the deep unhappiness you felt with her. And my heart broke. Has yours, Lucky? Did she break you?"

"Not like that, no. Michaela and me. Well, she was always honest, not interested in more than the fling, the sex, and us hanging out to talk about art. But that was it. And she told me all of that and I couldn't help but desire, lust for more, more from her. I did whatever she wanted, in the name of sex, I guess. But it wasn't enough. That's what broke me. Not her. Does that make sense?"

The fire was burning down, so I stood up, not waiting for an answer, but lighting candles, bringing in more wood. Chris went to the kitchen and found a bottle of Cabernet Sauvignon, and two glasses, mismatched but still, they were wine glasses.

"Can we?"

"Yeah, that's perfect. I haven't really been drinking much these days. But tonight, it sounds good."

"Are you sure? I don't want to be a bad influence!"

I smiled to myself, my young friend. I took the bottle from her and sat us both back down. I pulled some cushions over and made us a warm cozy den. Blue claimed a spot to my left, with Chris to my right.

"I understand. That's all I really wanted to say. I understand. And I'm okay with it, all that happened next door. I like you." She looked down suddenly. I took her hand in mine. We sat there, sipping wine, and staring into the fire.

Chris spoke first. "They're good!"

"What?" I broke out of my daydreams and looked at her.

"The photos. Of Michaela. Of you. Of me. They're good. You should show them!"

"Right!"

"No, seriously, I think you should show them. In Madison. With the others of the travels. They're erotic but so touching, too, human desire and pain and love. It works. Honest."

"Love?"

"Yeah, in the photos you took of me, in the moments you captured. In my eyes when I looked directly into the lens, and remember the ones of us at the park? On the swings? Yeah, well," she laughed and scratched her head. "At least, that's what I think."

I took her hand and stared into her eyes, searching for the truth of that. I found it.

Blue slept in the armchair.

45

I woke up to the fire barely glowing. Blue saw me and wagged her tail, climbed off her perch on the armchair, and came up to me. I patted her head, moved away from Chris, and tucked in the blankets behind me.

"Come on, girl. Let's make some coffee, shall we?"

She wagged her happy body and followed me. I walked into the kitchen and turned the lights on, closing the door behind me. Outside the sun was only just beginning to come up over the Sangre de Christos. Stripes of lemon yellow, mango and baby blue.

I put the teakettle on and noticed the empty bowl. I found Blue's dog food and set her up with breakfast. She ate happily, half watching me as she did, her tail tucked under as she concentrated. I stood next to the gas flame and looked around the room.

It was still very much Dad's home, but my living here had changed the place, even as simply as the way I'd arranged the mugs and teas and coffee pots. The plants were gone but I'd put up some frames full of photographs of the two of us, Dad and me. I'd even found more watercolor paintings he'd done ages ago, and they now hung on the wall behind me.

The water boiled and I poured it onto the coffee filter, and watched it, drip by drip. I thought I'd make a full pot later but first I needed some quiet time to myself. I didn't want to wake Chris.

Christmas was only days away. The doctor had told me this would be a benchmark for us. *How brain dead is he?*

I might have to close up his accounts, talk to lawyers, banks, and find my sister. It all hung on the next few days. I sipped the coffee and added a teaspoon of sugar.

I walked over to the fridge and had a look inside. It was fairly full, which took me by surprise. I hadn't been shopping. But someone had. Milk, cheeses, vegetables, and some homemade soups and stews lined the shelves.

I craved bacon and eggs. A real breakfast. Maybe I'd make some breakfast burritos? Yeah, that sounded perfect. I put on the coffee pot, enough for the both of us, and pulled out the pack of bacon, four free range eggs, the frozen Chimayo green chile. I hadn't cooked since being back; cheese on toast doesn't count, does it? The kitchen filled with smoke and good smells and soon enough, I heard Chris stirring. I brought her a mug with cream, no sugar. She laughed as Blue tried to claim a space on, or rather, under the blankets. I squatted down next to them both.

"I'm making breakfast. Do you want it in here or the kitchen?"

"Kitchen."

I stood and gave her a quick kiss on the lips. "It's almost ready."

"That was great, thanks, Lucky!" Chris sat back and rubbed her Buddha belly in appreciation. Blue licked the pan with a tail wagging. I sat back, full, and ready to face the day. "Do you want to come to the hospital with me? I'll be going there around midday if you're up for it. Come for the drive to Albuquerque—if you want, that is."

She nodded. "Of course I do. I want to meet your dad."

"You know how bad he is, though, right? He won't know you're there."

She nodded sadly. "I know. It's okay. I still want to come with you."

I took down one of the frames and showed her how we'd both been once upon a time, both of us skinny and tanned, hiking the mountains in Europe one summer. The Pyrenees. We'd spent a month learning Spanish and French as we went along, camping in the fields, and drinking red wine (him) and Coke (me) at the village bars in the heat of the day. Incredible views of snow capped peaks and valleys, watching all the animals that wandered the hills, the horses, donkeys, sheep, goats, pigs, you name it, and they all kept us company at one time or another.

Chris and I chatted about vacations as kids, hers in Upper Michigan on the lakes, mine in Europe. She laughed at the photograph of my scrawny little white legs poking out of shorts when I was in middle school. That damn English habit of making kids wear uniforms. I still hate ties.

I took the photo and stared at the image of Dad with his arm around my shoulders and me with a scowl on my face.

"Dad did his best. I didn't get it at the time—do we ever?" I shook my head. "I wish I could do it all again. Tell him. Tell him how much he gave me."

"You can. Now. Today. When we go to see him, just tell him, Lucky. We don't know how much longer you have with him, do we?"

"Not really. The doctors are worried that this it. That he's going to hang on for years like this. I'll have to find some kind of facility for him. How I do this, any of this, I don't know."

"No one you can ask?"

"Well, they have counselors and all, but I don't know. I'll deal with that later. Today, it's back to the hospital. Shall we call Mike and Susan, see if they want to meet you tonight? Come over here?"

I explained to her how they'd been coming over, and told the story of Mike finding Blue, and how we're just letting it all happen. They want to help. I need help. It works out, I said with a sheepish smile. She reached over the table to me and squeezed my hands. She sat back and looked up at the clock.

"Okay, I need a shower and then I'm ready. What else do you need help with?"

I looked down. "I still haven't been in Dad's room. Can you do that? Open it up, see what's there?"

"Yeah, let's do that tonight. You cook me dinner and I'll see what I can do."

We drove up Second Street, past the railroad tracks and across St Francis. She sat quietly, sharing the front bench with Blue. The window was open and the sun shone. Snow was expected for Christmas. I didn't care. The truck's heating blasted out and I relaxed for a moment. I waited at the lights, pointing out where the prairie dogs used to run wild.

"What happened?"

"When that new development was first planned, the papers ran all these stories, caused a huge uproar! Pretty amazing the lengths people went to. Anyway, they caught the prairie dogs and relocated them to south of town. But I bet that's now all being built up, too. It's out of sight, though, so there's no stories about the homeless buggers."

I smiled at the thought of such hypocrisies and drove up the road onto I-25 and we headed south. An hour later, I parked in the lower parking lot at the Veteran's Hospital, one of the best places in the State apparently, a teaching hospital with an amazing reputation. Dad was lucky to be there. Right.

The midday sun shone even though clouds were heading in. The weather was turning. Still, I covered the windows with the shade screen and cracked them each four or five inches. Got to let Blue get some fresh air. Besides, her breath stank.

"Dad, this is Christine. I told you about her."

I looked from one to the other. Chris's eyes flowed unchecked. Dad's face was swollen, from the medicine? His hair was unkempt, brushed, yes, but for practical reasons only. They'd shaved him as they usually did. His body was hooked up to various IVs and instruments that monitored and fed and hydrated him as needed. His body lay inert, lifeless and quiet, but for the sounds the machines made. The photograph on the shelf next to him was of Dad as an Officer in the '80s. I'd wanted the nurses to know how vital he'd been. The life force of the man that now lay in limbo before them.

Chris sat down shakily and clutched at my hand. I talked to Dad about finding her on the doorsteps the night before. I described how Blue took to Chris immediately.

"You'd like her, Dad. She's smart and pretty and funny. And she likes me! Funny, eh? She came all this way to meet you. From Madison. Chris, this is my Dad." I held his hand in mine. I turned to Chris and explained, "He raised me alone for so long. It's strange to be this side of the fence, taking care of him. He's getting his own back, I haven't been easy to care for, right, Dad?"

I chatted to them both, on and on, occasionally lapsing into silence. The nurses came and went. The doctor asked me to see her the following day, if possible. I nodded with a huge question mark across my forehead. She set a time for the afternoon, four o'clock. She told me to bring my family of friends if I wanted.

"I'll call them. Ask them. What shall I say?"

"Just that it's time we all talked about how he's doing and what we do next."

Chris looked down and stroked my Dad's fragile skin. Her tears fell on his wrist. I wanted to ask more, but Dr. Smith left us and started talking to the man in the bed next to us. She drew the curtains around them and the voices lowered.

46

Chris was working in Dad's room when Susan showed up with a grocery bag of goodies. Behind her stood a tall blond smiling man in less clothes than the weather demanded.

"David, right?"

"Yeah, how did you guess?"

I opened the door to them. They walked down the hallway, hand in hand, laughing about the stereotype Australian looks that David came with. That and his accent. Susan aimed for the kitchen and set him down at the table with a beer and then began to pack the food away. Cupboards. Fridge. Freezer. Countertops.

"I brought kale, figuring we haven't had any greens for a while. That okay with you?"

"Yep, but I was planning on cooking tonight."

"Really?" Susan stopped what she was doing in surprise. "Great! What are we having?"

David looked back and forth between us. "It's not a problem that I came along, is it? We don't plan on staying."

I came over and sat down near him. "No worries, mate!"

They both groaned at the bad attempt to copy his accent. I told them, "I'm thinking to make rice and a veggie stir fry. Kale would be great. Do we have enough for four of us?"

"Is Mike coming over?"

I reddened slightly. "No, Christine is here. She's back in Dad's room."

"Oh!" and with a huge grin, Susan headed off in that direction, taking a bottle of wine and two glasses with her. I started to stand up to follow but David passed me a bottle of Pale Ale and toasted me with a shrug. What could I do? I sat down and we listened. Or rather, we tried. Susan had closed the door. We waited, making small talk, the weather, and the radio station, that awkward we-don't-know-each-other small talk. Five minutes later, the girls returned to the kitchen.

"Oh, were you waiting for us?" asked Susan with a smile. Chris stood behind me and rested her hands on my shoulders, giving me a squeeze. I touched my fingertips to hers. "I was going to start cooking in a few minutes. Does someone want to call Mike? See if he's up for dinner with us?" I stood and made for the fridge.

"Sure." Susan picked up the phone.

"Can I help?" David finished his beer.

I asked him to set up the living room, make a fire, and find candles, that kind of thing. Chris leaned down. She gave me a fly-by kiss on the ear and told me how Susan's sudden entry into the bedroom had made her squeal out loud. She took a sip of my beer, and leaned against the counter by the sink. I found the onions, garlic, sweet corn, and greens and started chopping away. What a great smell. Of spring gardens. Susan passed me the fresh rosemary and dried thyme. Chris asked if I needed more help.

"No, believe it or not, I have it under control. Perhaps you could pick some music and put it on? The stereo is in the front room."

Susan got off the phone. She came over to me and mouthed the words *I like her* and then followed Chris and David out.

I was alone in the kitchen, Dad's kitchen, cooking for my friends. I could hear them chatting and laughing in the other room. I chopped and cut and sautéed. I drank a beer slowly. I wanted Dad here, to be here for this. But he wasn't. He liked gatherings, informal dinners with friends, his or mine. He liked cooking. Telling stories.

I put the rice on. I stirred the food. I stared out the darkened window. Finally it all came together. The food, that is. I laid the table for the four of us. I took the plates and a fork each, and set us up with fresh drinks, a candle in the middle of the kitchen table and I turned the lights lower.

"A toast!"

"Yeah, I think so." Mike pushed me to the side and found space enough for him at the table, dragging another chair over. Blue laid her head on my lap. We all held our glasses and bottles. They looked at me.

"Dad."

"To Bill."

We lay around the fireplace, full and happy. I lit some incense and another candle next to the photo of Dad from this last summer. He looked so happy. Up in the hills behind Tesuque, we'd gone for a walk with Blue; the trial followed the creek, heading toward a waterfall. She'd played in and out of the water, making us both jealous. I'd been the first to drop my jeans and join her. Then Dad followed. We sat in the water and chatted, taking photos of the incredible wildflowers, all the different kinds of penstamons, the sunflowers and the native grasses fluttering in the breeze. Birds flew past and one shit on Dad's shoulder. I'd laughed so hard that he dunked me under until I quit.

I came back to the conversation around me. David and Mike talked about the NFL games and their favorite teams, the Jets and the Steelers respectively. I hadn't kept up. The Saints were doing well, apparently. And the Packers had gotten three different coaches fired for bad performances against them. This was the gossip flowing over me. I had a rare cigarette.

"Lucky?"

Christine's voice called me from the bedroom. Dad's bedroom. She and Susan were cleaning up and airing it out.

"Yes?" I didn't want to move.

"I think you need to see this."

Mike and David looked at me. There was something about her tone that unnerved us all. I sat up. "Yeah?"

"Yes."

I stood up nervously. The guys sat there, watching me. No one said anything.

47

In the bedroom, the bed was made, but covered with suitcases and piles of odds and ends. The curtains were open, as were the windows. The heat was trying to keep up with the single digit temperatures outside. The light overhead had one burned out bulb. Must change that, I remember thinking. On the chair sat Susan, her face drawn, no words came out. Chris came up to me, holding a piece of paper. I took it but watched her eyes for some clue.

"Is what I think it is?"

I held the paper in my left hand, and fumbled nervously for the smokes with the other. I shook too much to do anything. I read the words once. My knees gave out and I fell onto the bed. I read the whole thing before looking up at them both. Susan and Christine. Their eyes watched me closely as I made the connection. Medical Power of Attorney. Lucky Phillips.

"He doesn't say what he wants, does he?" I reread the legal passages, trying to make sense of it all.

"Not really." Chris sat down, and put her hand on my leg and gave me a quick squeeze. "He just asks that you do the right thing for him, whatever you decide that is."

"So, I have the power? To decide? To decide whether he lives or dies?" I looked between them both.

"Yes, I'm afraid so."

"Oh, fuck."

I hung my head down, crumpling into a small ball. A kid. A selfish kid like me has to make that decision? How? How can I do that? Take a life? Dad's? I broke down. I sobbed my heart out, yelling out, and crying more than I knew was possible. They held me.

Blue came in and watched from the doorway, scared to come up to me. Mike and David stood beside her. I heard whispered explanations and the door closing behind Susan as she left me with Christine. I couldn't move. The room was in shadows. The paintings on the wall mesmerized me. I didn't blink. I stared.

I curled up on my Dad's bed, half covered in a blanket, a candle burning on the bedside table, his books and reading glasses still lying there. I held myself close. I rocked back and forth. I had no words. Chris laid me down on Dad's bed. She pulled back the covers and took my boots off, my socks, and my jeans. She tucked me under the sheets. She found the old teddy bear on the shelf and rested him next to me, facing me. I said nothing. I did nothing. She turned the light off and left me alone with my memories. Blue jumped up and lay at my feet, staring at me.

"Come here, girl."

She crawled up the bed until she reached me, face next to mine and then she licked away my tears. We fell asleep.

48

We met the staff en masse. Chris held onto the files. The will. All of it. With the two of us came Susan and David, Mike and Blue. But Blue stayed in the truck. I'd wanted to bring her in with me, to say goodbye.

I looked a wreck, with red eyes, swollen from the night before. Shaky from lack of food and too much coffee and nicotine, I stood in my clean clothes, a new dark gray cotton shirt, black jeans and my inevitably dirty work boots. My hands shook. I stuffed them in my pockets.

Chris looked drained, her fair skin paler than usual. Silent, we all sat in the Family room, not talking to each other, just waiting for the hospital staff to talk to us, all ten of us squashed in together. I hated it. I stared out the window. I ignored everyone. I sipped the black coffee. Paperwork was handed around.

At some point, Dr Smith sent me down alone to the meditation room. "It's just a chapel room set aside for those in need of contemplation. Like right now. Go take a moment for yourself. We'll wait."

I shrugged and left everyone in there. I went down the side steps and found it as promised. A place to sit and focus. For Muslims, Buddhists and Christians alike. I sat on the bench and hung my head. I stared at the snow falling outside. The sun peeked through a cloud. I could see my truck and Blue's little nose was resting on the doorframe, staring at the hospital doors. Blue. Dad.

Dad.

Back in the room, I made my decision. We talked about practical issues, what to expect and how to take care of ourselves. There was no way of knowing how long he'd live once the machines were taken away. The hospital's decision was made after three hours of pretty detailed, intense discussion. Dr. Smith agreed with me, that it was time to let Dad go, but she had to play devil's advocate. She had to make sure we all agreed before the paperwork would be finished.

"Are you sure that turning off the life support is the right thing to do, Lucky? I'm not talking about the legal issues, but how do you feel about the right to life? Ethical and religious reasons are there for situations like this. We don't have to give you all the power. I can find loopholes in such a will. It's up to you."

"It's time."

"Time to what?"

"To let him die. This is selfish of us to keep him like this. I can't watch it any more. He's not coming back, is he?"

They all shook their heads, and then someone described palliative care to me, the pain meds, and the focus of how they'll be there with him for however long it took. Each of them cared. That was so incredibly obvious to me.

One young nurse excused herself, with tears in her eyes. But the doctors talked more and more, of what they had seen in Dad's MRI results, the patterns of pneumonia, and lack of response to stimulus. Susan asked questions. Mike was as silent as me. We caught each other's eye at one point and he stared but did nothing, said nothing.

I signed the papers.

We were allowed to visit Dad, all of us, but one at a time. The nurses asked us to come back later. They had to move him to another room. A private room, calm and quiet, no more machines or tests or any of that. A room for goodbyes.

I was the last to leave. I held his hand and looked around this ward I knew so well. The instruments, the sheets, the televisions silent in the corners, the view out to the hills, and the other patients who came and went. I knew it so well. I was scared to leave it. To leave Dad.

They didn't know. That was the final say. No one knew how long he'd take. How long until his body let go and he died. Every breath could be the last. There was nothing solid or certain about any of this. It was up to him now. I held his hand and whispered goodbye, over and over.

"It's okay now, Dad. It's time to go. Don't worry about me. Blue is back. I wish you could have seen her one more time. She's with me now, Dad. I have my best friend." I laughed softly. "I have Mike back, too. Susan. And Christine is here now. I'm okay, Dad. Don't stay because of me. I'll find my sister. I promise. I'll tell her all about you. The travels and the stories. I'll take her the photos I found. I'll give her one of your paintings, too, okay? Don't worry about me, Dad. Take care of yourself now."

I kissed his mouth gently. I stroked his hair back. I put his hand back down. I said goodbye again and again. I couldn't leave.

I spent the next few days coming and going. I don't know how many. I'd wake up at home and in his bed, wrap his robe around me, and go to make coffee. Chris slept alone in my room and usually appeared as soon as the coffee smell woke her. We took Blue for walks at the dog park off West Alameda. I'd go to Albuquerque and sit with Dad. Chris cooked at the house, took care of things, and brought food to the hospital. I sometimes fell asleep next to Dad, with my head resting next to his hand. I spent all the time I could with him.

They'd moved him to a corner room, with windows both south and west. I kept the windows slightly cracked so we could get fresh air. The nurses took care of us all, no longer needing to protect Dad from too many visitors; we were all allowed to stay for as long as we liked.

I had the mornings to myself. Chris stayed with me in the afternoons. Mike and Susan came around six or so. Mostly I just sat by Dad and talked to him. The good and the bad stories both. I told him about shames, pains, and yes, the ways I've laughed over the last few years. How I'd pulled up outside the biker's bar, the Mineshaft in Madrid, with my beat up old Yamaha 750, only to drop it as everyone stood on the porch watching me. I'd had to ask for help, much to their derision. Some older white guy, a local with a beard and no front teeth finally came down and helped me.

I told Dad how jealous I'd been of that damn baby Alpaca in Spain! I talked about the photography show in Madison, how I'd met Daniel and taken photos of everyone I'd met driving cross-country. I asked him what I should do, should I go up there, anyway? Would I have the time? I told him I didn't want the attention. Not now. I remembered more stories of Mom and I told him what came to me. How she'd made chicken soup on Sundays and drank red wine on

Wednesdays, listening to Oldies on the radio. I talked and talked. I said everything I needed to say. Dad lay there. I watched him slowly releasing and relaxing. It was magical.

The doctor came in and nodded to me as she picked up the medical notes. She read in silence. It was just me for once. The sky darkened as the storm raged and snow fell fast and hard.

"Do you want to bring your dog inside?" I

looked up, startled. "What?"

"Do you want to go get your dog? What's her name?"

"Blue. But how did you know?"

She smiled softly. "I've been around you for almost a month now, Lucky. I notice a lot. And well, I've seen you go out and walk her around every few hours. She's a pretty girl. Well behaved by the looks of it."

I perked up and talked of how we'd lost her and how Mike found her for me. I told her that Dad and I'd adopted her together six years ago, from the shelter south of Santa Fe. We chatted and she sat down opposite me, with Dad between us, and we talked about our animal friends.

"Dogs are amazing, aren't they? And I don't mean just our friends like Blue is for you or Gerry is for my partner and me. But we have trained Companion Dogs here, too, they come visit the patients."

"So we really can bring her in? To visit Dad?"

Dr. Smith said, "Yes, we'll pretend she's trained. If anyone asks, tell them I sent for Blue to visit a hospice patient. All above board."

We sat there, looking at each other and she smiled. "I know how terrible this is, but it's the right thing to do, isn't it?" She watched Dad breathing, slowly and unsteadily. He suddenly stopped, as if he'd forgotten what he was doing, and we stared at him. A deep breath followed. Unnerved, I nodded, afraid to use my voice.

"It's time to say goodbye, Lucky. I don't think your Dad will make another night."

She stood up and I did the same. We looked down at him sleeping, lost in his own world.

"Let's get your four-legged friend, shall we?"

49

Kate, the doctor that is, came out with me and, bundled up in our winter coats, we headed out to the truck and called to Blue. Her head popped up and she looked around for me. She stood up with her whole body wagging. The windows were fogged up and covered with fresh snow. I let her out and she ran around excitedly with her snout digging trenches and kicking up the flakes as she pranced and showed off for us both. I went to pull out a cigarette but no longer really wanted one. I threw them into the back of the truck bed. I grabbed Blue's leash from the front seat and called to her. Kate had just thrown a snowball that Blue caught with a leap and yelp of surprise when it fell apart in her mouth.

"Come on, girl. Let's go."

Blue ran up and sat next to me. I put the leash on her and then she started pulling me toward the building. Never did quite get around to teaching her not to pull. I almost slipped face-first into a snow bank. I thought of Michaela. I needed to call her. Frank. I should write. I should—there was so much I should do. Later.

Kate led the way. We took the steps up and came in next to the security guards.

"Hi, how's the weather forecast?" asked Dr. Smith as we passed them at the main stairwell. They chatted to her about the storm that was expected to last for the rest of the Christmas holidays. A thick cold front hovered over the state. As we closed the door behind us, Kate explained that normally new Companion Dogs had to show all their shots and training certificates. She'd happily distracted them.

Blue was quiet, calmer now. She stuck close to my side. The smells of the hospital made her uneasy. We walked past the sanitation stations and we washed our hands, as usual. Blue sat at next to me and watched as the doctor and I chatted softly. The windows showed low glowing skies and an almost empty parking lot. The hallway had various stretchers and wheelchairs lined along the far wall, with boxes of supplies waiting to be unpacked. Christmas cards were stuck to the notice board.

We opened the door to Dad's room and the doctor called out to him.

"I've brought Lucky back to say goodbye, Bill. We have Blue with us. Remember Blue? She wanted to give you a lick or two before you leave us."

Blue stood, staring at this familiar body but he had the wrong smells. She didn't want to get closer.

"It'll take a moment for her. Let's close the door and take her off leash, okay, Lucky?" She looked more carefully at me. "You okay?"

I nodded and did as she asked. Blue slowly walked forward, following me, until I sat at my usual seat. I reached for Dad's hand and sat down, talking to him about the roads and the snow still falling. I told him about us sneaking in Blue to see him.

"She's a bit nervous of you, Dad. Funny, eh? She used to sleep on the dog bed next to yours, waking whenever you did. I guess you smell different. Hey, Blue. It's Dad. Come here, girl."

She trusted me and I held his hand to her nose. Her tail wagged slowly, uncomprehending. But then she licked him and she looked me in the eyes.

"Yes, it's Dad. Want to come here?"

I patted my lap and she jumped up, curled up, all forty-five pounds of her, and she stared straight into his face. Her body slumped against me. We sat there and I talked to them both.

"I'll leave you now, Lucky. Go back out the same way, using those stairs. The guards will know you now so it won't be a problem. Take your time." Kate touched my shoulder briefly. "And, Bill. You take care and let them say goodbye. It's time for you to pass on, so be brave. We'll miss you." And she touched his face gently.

We sat there, Blue and me, for hours, well into the late night. The snow continued to fall. I talked every once in a while. Blue licked his hand. I leaned back and dozed as I stared at him breathing. The doctor was right. He had almost gone; I could feel it.

"Dad, it's okay. I'll be okay. I have my friends around me. You need to let go now. It's time to go."

After a while, I patted the bed and Lucky jumped across from my lap, and lay so gently at his side. She looked at me and at him, then started to wash his face. She lay with her head on his chest. I took out my camera.

"Can I, Dad?"

Blue wagged her tail.

I set the camera up on the table behind me, facing Dad and the snow-filled window. Blue watched me. I aimed it at the two of them. The tears streamed down my face, making it hard to focus. I pressed the self-timer. I sat in my usual chair and held Dad's hand. Blue reached and licked his cheek. I stared at them both, tears unchecked.

Click.

Finally, it was time to leave him. I couldn't stay any longer. I just couldn't. I took Blue off the bed and put the leash on her. I kissed him goodbye one last time. We walked to the door. I turned back.

"Bye, Dad. I love you. I'll miss you."

I turned out the lights.

50

The drive up the interstate took all my focus. The windshield wipers fought with the snowstorm. I could barely see. A whiteout. The lanes lay hidden under barely touched snow, inches thick. It was hell what with the weather, the lights and me sobbing.

Blue lay on the bench seat with her head on my lap. I had the window wide open. It was freezing. How late was it? I had no idea. The streets were empty. Two hours later and sixty miles driven, I finally took St. Francis without a problem, but I saw tracks of other cars that'd slipped and slid. The clouds hung low and heavy. Turning onto San Mateo, I drove past the brewery and their lights were on, but hardly any cars lined the street. I drove another block and turned right onto Dad's road. The house was lit up and cars in the driveway. Mike's and Susan's, by the looks of it. I pulled up next to the Chevy and parked. Blue sat up.

"Want to go for a walk?"

She stood, half across me, anxious to run in the cold fun stuff. I opened the door and rolled the window up. I locked the truck. I walked down the street and took a right and then a left. We walked in the middle of the roads, empty but for a few car tracks, not much activity. I was silent. I had nothing to say. Nothing. Empty. My head and heart were so empty.

Silently, I walked up the railroad trail until we hit Second Street again and we turned back to Dad's. Blue ran. I walked with my cold feet, hands deep in my coat pockets. I stared up, face to the flakes. I ate three. I walked. I watched Blue run and play and dig and jump and fall over. Wiped out completely, she stood up and looked around as if embarrassed. I laughed. Out loud. I laughed.

Chris stood at the sink, pouring out a pan of hot water. She looked over quickly and smiled. "I'm making mashed potatoes. We have roast chicken and some greens and Susan is making gravy. Mike's around somewhere."

I nodded and went into Dad's room. I closed the door. I sat on his bed and hung my head and just sat there for a moment. The room hadn't changed. I took off my wet clothes and changed into pajamas and his robe, thick and a deep red, I snuggled into it, smelling his aftershave again. I stood up and opened the door to my friends.

At the table, we all sat, the four of us. Mike had put on Afro Celt Sound System. Susan had lit a couple of candles and put a framed photo of Dad between them. The table was laid with piles of food, even bowls of nuts, fruit, cheese and crackers. Mike and Susan chatted as they poured out wine for each of us. I sat quietly in Dad's chair at the head of the table, facing the window to the back yard. Chris came and sat next to me, reached out and held my hand. She looked at the others.

"Ready?"

They nodded and put the glasses down. We held hands around the table. I looked at each of them, one by one. Smiles and tears both. We didn't need to say anything. Blue rested her head on my lap. I nodded one last time.

"Hungry, anyone?"

We tucked in and they all started chatting. I told them of taking Blue into the ward, and of the drive home. I listened in to their stories of chaos in town and at work over the last few days. Christmas fever had hit town.

The wine began to flow. Susan turned the lights down, the music up. Chris cleaned up the table. Mike opened another bottle of merlot.

I sat back and looked around the living room. The paintings on the walls. The snow outside on the elms and pinion trees. The fireplace held us warm. Candles on the sideboards. I looked over at the photo of my Dad. Henry William Phillips.

I looked at this family of mine. Chris. Mike. Susan. And of course, Blue. They were chatting about other Christmas holidays they'd had over the years, laughing at Mike's tales of Europe, and drinking the wine for breakfast.

In this warm cozy home of mine, I realized: I'm Lucky. Lucky to be alive.

PART THREE

51

I sat next to the table with the wine, sipping at a cabernet sauvignon when a hand touched my shoulder. Michaela stood over me. She smiled wickedly and gave me a big sloppy kiss on the cheek. She stood with her back to the crowds and toasted me with her glass of chardonnay. She wore a simple black dress and big black boots that emphasized her tall lean frame, small hips and the slight curves of her breasts. Her hair was loose, hanging down across her shoulders. She looked stunning and knew it. I stood up next to her and hugged her back.

"Congratulations, Lucky. This is an amazing success," and her eyes twinkled as she continued, "I'm so glad I inspired all these great photos!"

I groaned and laughed both. "I couldn't have done it without you."

"I'm sorry about your dad, though." She touched me gently on the cheek. "Let me know if I can help, okay?"

I nodded my thanks. Michaela looked away when she saw my eyes tear up, and we checked out what was happening in the gallery. I'd had no idea it'd be like this.

The place was packed. What with the noise of everyone chatting and laughing, the guitarist strumming flamenco over by the front door, and the sound of champagne bottles popping, it was deafening. Overwhelming. And absolutely heartwarming.

I'd talked for the last two hours with whomever James and John introduced to me, shaking hands, talking of those journeys we all crave, listening politely to their opinions of my photos, and now I was drained. Utterly drained. It had been a long week. Month, I guess. Months.

The landscape paintings were all gone and the walls were lined with my work. My work. What a concept! In all, John and James had taken thirty-five photographs and framed them for the show. They had chosen, printed, and organized everything in my absence. Apparently, Christine and Michaela had been in touch, and the gallery knew what was going on at the hospital the whole time, and well, that took care of that. The releases were signed and delivered.

John's expression once he realized his Professor of a sister was the model for some of the more erotic images was to be told and retold. Michaela didn't seem to mind the infamy, anything but. She told me that the other teachers in the English Department were jealous. Donald, her lover, included. I'd talked to James earlier this week, once everything had slowed down in Santa Fe and I finally gave him the titles for the pieces. No names as requested by the subjects. All I had to do was show up. I did. With Christine, Mike and his new girlfriend Laura, the bartender from the Cowgirl at home, and Susan had brought David. Blue stayed home with a neighbor, I couldn't put her on a plane, knowing I'd be back in less than a week. I just couldn't. But I missed my best friend at my side, now I had no excuse to walk away when needed.

Chris stood off to one side, taking care of her own project. She took off her thick winter coat and wore the grey and green striped sweater I'd lent her last week. Her hair was growing longer again and it stuck out in all directions. The table near the door had been cleaned off of everything but the framed photographs of Dad, Mom, and even some of myself as a kid. Chris had even brought back the two brass candlesticks from Dad's house and put them with the photos, lighting long red candles once the opening officially began. I had added a picture of Blue. Chris chatted away to James as she put the photos back in place after handing them to him to be seen in close up. James refused to wear his glasses in public.

James told me of being pleased with the turn out. He kept checking the room for new potential customers, and wandered off to shake hands and schmooze. He did it well. Jennifer, still happy to be working at the gallery, poured the wine and took down the details of people's interests in various prints, and even placed little red stickers on those that sold. Joanna came in, and I stared at her uncertainly. She smiled warily and came closer. She simply gave me a hug. No words needed.

Behind me, Mike talked to Michaela, thrilled to be here. His face was flushed, smiling widely, and his girlfriend was holding his hand, half hiding from all.

"We made it! Only just, though, that last drive from Chicago was a killer, what with the New Year traffic and the snowstorm. Lucky did great, though! Got used to bad driving in New Mexico the last few weeks. I fell asleep, didn't I?"

They were standing in front of the image of Michaela reaching for me, a blurred naked body hidden by the arm stretching toward the camera.

"Who's that? She's beautiful!" Laura stepped closer to inspect the details.

Michaela smiled smugly at me and chatted to Mike about the trip. I walked around the room, nodding and making small talk. I really had little to say.

"Lucky?" a shaky voice brought me out of myself. Daniel and Frank sat on the bench near the office, both struggled to get up, but I waved them down and joined them. We sat in a line and watched the people coming and going, the social whirlwind that the opening was.

A flash took me by surprise. Angela, the journalist, stood in front of the three of us with her camera in hand. "I hope you don't mind. You all looked so thoughtful. It was quite a beautiful image."

Frank shook her hand and introduced himself. "I'm in the one over there, the handsome older man under the lamp. You can have my autograph later, when you interview me, that is!"

Angela laughed and offered to do that right now, if he'd be so kind. They wandered off to find a quiet table. Daniel and I watched them for a moment. He turned to me with a soft smile.

"I heard from your young lady about your Dad. I'm sorry, Lucky. But I'm glad you went back."

I nodded. "Me, too."

"When is the memorial?"

"Next week. We go back on Monday and then we get together with his friends on Thursday. Christine's coming back for that but then she has to be here for school. It's all a bit rushed. I'm living in New Mexico for now, and she's still in school here. It's strange timing, isn't it? To meet someone?"

He nodded and patted me on the knee. "That's life, though, isn't it? Did you ever find your sister?"

"No, that's next. I'll try to find her before the memorial, but I don't see it happening, to be honest. If I find her, I'll take her some of Dad's things in the spring. I don't know. But I know I want to meet her, at least once. I promised Dad I'd do my best." I paused for a moment. Quiet. Then I turned back to Daniel and explained. "Family. She's my family. I'll find her."

He nodded and I remembered the photograph he'd given me. John came up to us, dressed impeccably as always, and he dragged me politely away and to the front of the room. I looked back at Daniel and saw him stand up and talk to Christine. They both headed our way. A tired but happy smile crossed her face as she waved. I relaxed.

John stood tall and tapped his wine glass. Susan and David pushed their way to the front line and she toasted me. David muttered something that made her giggle. John carried on with a frown at their disruption and tapped his glass again. The buzz lessened and he spoke.

"I'd like to introduce you all to Lucky Phillips. This is the Lucky Shot candid portrait show, a tale, a journey we've all dreamt of taking, but Lucky had the drive to follow it through. We only just got Lucky here in time today so, please everyone, let's hear it for our newest talent!"

A round of cheers went up to the rooftop. John turned to me and invited me to say something. I shook inside but turned to face the crowd. The gallery spot lights shone on the photographs, on these unknown visitors, and on my friends. I took a deep breath and let it out slowly.

"This has been an intense process, to get to this point. It's been a rough year to say the least. Anyway, I'd like to thank each of you for coming out here tonight. It's pretty bad outside, right? Quite the storm on the way up here from O'Hare. Well anyway, we didn't come here to talk about the weather, did we? It's New Year's Eve and it seems a perfect way to start afresh, doesn't it? The snow suits the mood and it suits the show, it's a clean start for me, for all of us. Oh, and before I forget, I'd like to thank my models, whether they knew it or not, they all gave me inspiration on this journey."

Mike poked Christine and she blushed. Michaela drank back her wine with a smirk.

I carried on. "I'd like to thank John and James and Jennifer for all their work. All of you. But mostly, I'd like to dedicate tonight to the memory of my dad. Let's toast him, shall we? Henry William Phillips, a pain in my ass and I'll miss him like crazy!"

"Henry William Phillips!"

I toasted them all. The champagne corks flew, the flamenco music kicked in, the candles flickered and voices called out Dad's name and mine. Mike teased me for my first public speech being so short, not funny enough by his reckoning. That's friends for you. I punched him on the shoulder and he grinned. I shook hands with John. Chris was walking toward me. Michaela stood chatting to Daniel. I looked around once more. I took out my camera and shot from the hip.

Click.

CONTINUED IN THE NOVEL

LUCKY FIND

Lucky and Mike, best friends since childhood, travel through New Mexico and into Arizona, accompanied by Blue, a collie mix. Looking for Lucky's newly discovered half-sister, these friends search across the Southwest, including visits to Las Cruces, Bisbee, and Flagstaff. The clues they follow begin resembling something an undercover genealogist might dream up. Over the weeks, Lucky unscrambles the past, one that challenges stereotypes of family, friendships, and gender, while laying a few good secrets to rest. Meanwhile, Blue, being a most generous dog, embarks on her own search and rescue mission, finding a needing-to-be-bottle-fed pup aptly named Peanut. It's the two dogs - and soon Blue's tiny kitten foundlings - that give this archetypal hero's journey a mixture of heartbreak and comic lightness.

http://amzn.com/1625166397

Also Available by Sarah Leamy

When No One's Looking
Fiction. 210 pages. $13.50

"*When No One's Looking* makes me homesick for the simple, hardscrabble, poetic life that unfolds daily in the Ortiz Mountains of New Mexico—and for the raw, fearless emotions and journeys of its people, as brought to life in Sarah Leamy's protagonist Joey. It's a story about the outer and inner landscapes that lead to love, to hate, and ultimately to wisdom."

—Carol Carpenter, playwright

An engagingly written novel that spans six countries and over 40 years, the story centers on an obsessive pair of lovers who cannot stay away from each other. Joey and Kat have had a messy relationship dating back to 1967. We follow their mis-adventures from a small town in New Mexico, then to Central America, Spain, Russia, the United Kingdom, and back to New Mexico. Looking back over the years, Joey reminisces with best friend, Paula on what could have been, while planning a final gathering of friends and family.

http://amzn.com/1507618441

Winner of the New Mexico/ Arizona Fiction Award 2012.

BRING A CHAINSAW

Travel memoirs. 278 pages.

Have you ever wondered what it's like to clean up after a hurricane in Florida? Where those dirt roads in Colorado will take your broken heart? How to build an adobe and straw-bale home by hand? How to keep your mouth shut when living at a Buddhist monastery in England? What it's like to be a volunteer firefighter? Or what to wear for your first day at Clown School? These stories and many more bring the reader into the alternative cultures in the States and Europe both, as you wander the many roads that brought her from Worcestershire, England to a small village in Northern New Mexico's mountains.

http://amzn.com/1523359854

LIVING THE DREAM

Fiction. 278 pages.

Jenny, a teacher from Olympia, WA moves to New Mexico with her musician boyfriend. They decide to give up all the conveniences of the city and follow the dream of an off-grid, sustainable and trendsetting green lifestyle in a small rural community. Just the thing to spice up their relationship, and cheaper than having a kid. They arrive in the high desert, following the GPS directions, and struggle to find the forty acres and the RV. Quickly humbled by how little prepared they are, they try to settle in within this unique small town. Only it's not as easy as the magazines make it seem.

http://amzn.com/1503107728

About the Author

Sarah Leamy was the boring little sister who suddenly left her English life and became the broke nomadic wanderer and writer. She finally
settled in New Mexico in her late twenties although she's still taking extended road trips when she can. As the socially awkward and insecure Brit abroad, she lived first in Europe and then crossed the States and into Guatemala, performing, writing and working odd jobs as she explored
new countries alone or with Daisy, her slightly grumpy Border Collie. Since then her stories, poems, essays and articles have been published in numerous online magazines, in newspapers, anthologies, and also in London, Madison, San Francisco and New Mexico. Her second novel
won Best Fiction in the 2012 New Mexico/ Arizona Book Awards, and was a finalist with her third, Lucky Find. These days she's become more known as the odd Englishwoman with the dogs who lives in the mountains near Santa Fe, suddenly appearing with another novel in hand.

Author's website:

www.dirtroadsanddogs.wordpress.com

Manufactured by Amazon.ca
Acheson, AB